THE
Quicksand Pony

THE
Quicksand Pony

ALISON LESTER

ALLEN&UNWIN
SYDNEY·MELBOURNE·AUCKLAND·LONDON

This paperback edition published in 2012

First published in 1997

Copyright © Text and Photographs, Alison Lester 1997

Allen & Unwin
83 Alexander Street
Crows Nest NSW 2065
Australia
Phone: (61 2) 8425 0100
Fax: (61 2) 9906 2218
Email: info@allenandunwin.com
Web: www.allenandunwin.com

A Cataloguing-in-Publication entry is available from the
National Library of Australia
www.trove.nla.gov.au

ISBN 978 1 74237 800 8

Cover and text design by Ruth Grüner
Cover photo by Getty Images / Sally Crossthwaite
This book was printed in November 2011 at McPherson's Printing Group,
76 Nelson St, Maryborough, Victoria 3465, Australia.
www.mcphersonsprinting.com.au

1 3 5 7 9 10 8 6 4 2

IN MEMORY OF DON

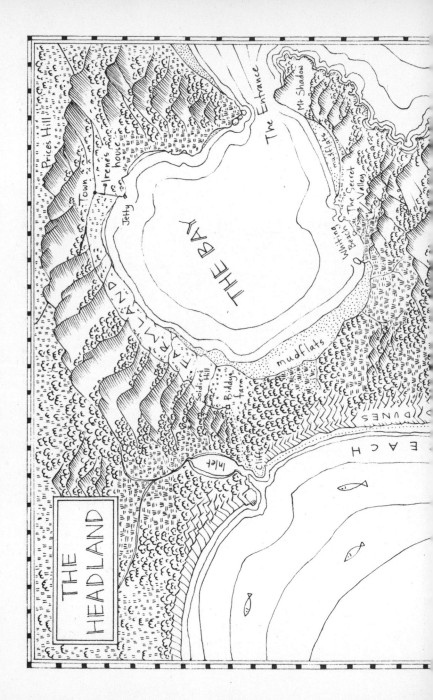

I

The disappearance

The moon was full the night they disappeared. Windswept paddocks lay clear and blue under high tatters of cloud. A car lurched, without lights, along the rutted road that ran from the town to the bay. It moved erratically, urgently, as though the driver didn't know how to drive. The wind whipped away the sound of the engine.

At the landing the car bumped to a stop and a slim figure emerged. She moved quickly, ferrying her bags and boxes into a dinghy moored at the ricketty bush jetty. Finally, satisfied that the oars and gear were right, she returned to the car and lifted out another bundle which she carried with great tenderness to the boat. She stowed it carefully in the bow, away from the wind and spray, then slipped into the boat like a cat and rowed silently out with the swirling tide.

The boat moved across the bay, through the shadows of scudding clouds. The tide was rushing out, rushing towards the entrance of the bay and beyond to the wild open sea.

She had to row across the current to reach the headland on the other side. She settled into a steady rhythm of rowing. If she kept the lights of the town lined up with the top of Price's Hill, she'd be on the right line.

The waves slapped against the side of the boat, uneven and choppy. It became more difficult to row. Her right oar missed the water altogether, as the dinghy pitched, and sent her sprawling backwards. She was drenched with spray, and there were hours of rowing to go. Oh for a bit of flat water.

It was a desperate struggle. If she rested for a moment the tide snatched the boat and dragged it towards the entrance. It was hard to tell how long she'd been rowing. She twisted on the wooden seat to look at the headland. She wasn't even halfway, but she was already tired and her hands were blistered from the rough wooden oars.

I'm never going to make it, she thought. It's too hard with the wind and the tide against me. Everything was

always against her. She rested the oars on her knees and dropped her head in despair, then looked up as she felt the boat shift against the tide.

The east wind, the easterly they always cursed for the bad weather it brought, had come to her help. It swung around from the south-west, gusting and ruffling the water, and pushed the dinghy towards the mountains.

It was going to be all right. Her hands weren't so sore. Her chest didn't feel as if it was about to burst any more. She could do it.

She lifted the edge of the tarpaulin in the bow and listened intently. Not a sound. She smiled and began to row again.

The lights of the town became smaller and smaller. Across the silver water on her left (her port side, she thought) the farms that lay between the town and the headland were in darkness. Everyone would have been in bed long ago. Some of the dairy farmers would probably be getting up soon to milk their cows. The boat inched across the bay, its wake fanning out behind. She was mesmerised by the moving water. Images flicked through her mind. She thought of everything. She thought of nothing. She kept on rowing.

One of the oars banged against the side of the boat and she grabbed it with a start. Had she been asleep, or just dreaming? She looked over her shoulder. There was the beach, Whiting Beach. She was almost there.

The girl gave one last pull on the oars, to ground the boat in the shallows, and then lay back against the seat, breathing in ragged gasps.

Her baby started to cry. She fished him out of his blanket, held him to her breast and fed him. As he nursed she listened to the waves lapping on the sheltered shore and knew she had come home. Far across the moonlit bay the lights of the town were no more than a sparkling chain.

She was never going back.

It took her all night to clear their gear off the beach and get rid of the boat without leaving a trace. Her brother and dad were both trackers, and they would be desperate to find her. They'd be worried sick. Still, she had to do this. Had to get away from the town and come out here to grieve, to rest. Later on she'd let them know she was okay.

She dragged the boat through the shallows to where a

low granite slab ran down to the sea. They couldn't track her on rock. She unloaded her boxes and bags. Then she left the baby sleeping in his blanket, wedged between her jumper and boots, and rowed the dinghy along the shore to the point. When she felt the current begin to tug, she slipped overboard, gave the boat a shove into the rip, and waded back around the bay. Her dress felt wet and heavy against her legs. Without stopping she gathered up the dripping fabric and wrung it out, then tucked the skirt under her waistband, clear of the water. The wind brushed over her wet skin, but she didn't feel cold. There was a gentleness and warmth on this beach that made her heart feel lighter already.

Carefully, so carefully, not leaving a footprint, a snagged thread, a broken twig, she carried her baby and the first load up the rock, then waded into the creek and followed it to the hidden valley she remembered from so long ago. It was her secret place, the place she'd discovered to hide in when her mother had died.

2

Almost nine years later

The farmhouse nestled against a low ridge of banksias, with a glassed-in porch that faced north to catch the winter sun. The paint on the window frames and roof had faded, and in the evening light looked pink against the white-washed weatherboards. A silvered paling fence ran crookedly around the garden, giving the flowers and vegetables shelter from the salt winds that blasted in from the strait. Ragged cypresses leaned over the shed near the house, and from her bed Biddy could hear their branches scraping against the roof.

The sun had just gone down and night was slowly overtaking the colours of the landscape. To the north-east a few lights marked farmhouses scattered along the coastal plain, and beyond that, way off, were the lights of the town. High purple hills cupped the bay, then petered out behind the farm.

The other way there were no lights, just miles of bush rolling around the bay, with the headland rising from it like an island.

Biddy thought she lived in the perfect spot, with the town on one side, the headland on the other, and the bay in front. Sometimes she rode up to the gravel ridge behind the stockyards and planned how she would defend her kingdom if she were a princess.

Their farm was at the end of the road, the furthest away from town. Biddy's grandfather had cleared the land and now her parents farmed it, grazing cattle and sheep. They had a small breeding herd of Hereford cows, but their main business was fattening cattle. Every

autumn they bought young steers, when the prices were low, and put them to winter on the headland, a run of wild country the family had leased since the 1920s. The sweet native grasses that grew in the gullies made the cattle fat and sleek. Now, in the spring, was the time to sell them.

It took two days to muster and drive the cattle home along the beach, and Biddy had never been allowed to go. She always had to stay home with Grandpa. She really wanted to go this year.

Biddy listened, straining her ears for a distant sound, but there were too many other noises. The house creaked and shifted in the wind. Over at the big shed a loose sheet of iron banged and rattled. In the next room Grandpa's radio crackled out the weather report, and Tigger, stretched on her bed, was purring like an engine.

She knelt beside the window and pressed her face hard up against the glass. There was just the black swirling night. Nothing. Hang on, yes, there was a flash of light over on Soldier's Hill. Yes. It was . . . it was a cattle truck all right. They were easy to pick, with lights all along the trailer.

'Dad! Dad! Marty Reed is here with the new cows, our new breeding cows! I saw him coming down the hill!'

'Good on you, mate. I'll go and help him unload. Those old girls have been on the road all day, so they'll be pretty thirsty and tired.'

'Can I come, Dad? Can I? Please? Go on, I won't—'

'All right, Bid, all right. But put a jumper on over your pyjamas. It's pretty cold.'

The truck was already backed up to the loading race when they reached the yards, and the driver waved from the gate.

'Hey, it's me girlfriend! How are ya, toots?'

Biddy had a huge crush on Marty Reed, even though he was twenty-four, and more than twice her age. He was tall and skinny, like a reed, and wore his pants so low on his hips that his shirt went forever before it tucked in. She gave him a hasty wave and climbed through the fence to see her pony. Bella was so white she seemed to glow against the dark yards. She nuzzled Biddy's neck as the girl buried her face in the silver mane.

'You might as well throw a bridle on her, Bid,' called her father. 'You can drive the cows over the road for me.'

Bella still had some of her winter coat. She felt soft and furry through Biddy's flannelette pyjamas, and easy to grip on to. Biddy grabbed a handful of mane anyway. It would be a bummer to fall off in front of Marty Reed.

She rode away from the glow of the headlights, to guide the mob across the road and into their paddock. She felt like a bushranger . . . Maybe she was a cattle duffer sneaking this mob down to the headland, to hide out in the bush and wait for them to have their calves. They'd be so sweet, with their fluffy tails. She'd have to—

'Look out!' Suddenly a black shadow leapt out, barking, as the cows neared the gateway. They wheeled, bellowing, and tore away down the road. Bella raced after them before Biddy had time to think. She could hear her father cursing Nugget. 'You useless mongrel of a dog! If they get up to the main road . . .! By God I'll give you a . . .'

Bella galloped along the gravel track. Biddy could hear the cows crashing through the scrub on the road-side, but she couldn't see them. It was so dark she could barely see the trees against the sky. 'Whoa!' she called. 'Whoa, old cows!'

Over the first hill the bush thinned, and as Bella raced

to head off the cows their white faces showed dimly in the night. Gradually they began to slow down, responding to Biddy's calming voice. 'Come on, girls, let's go home. Come on . . . ho . . . get up . . . that's the way.' Finally they turned around and moved back through the scrub with Biddy and Bella following them. Biddy's pyjamas were soaked with the pony's sweat, and she could hear the cows panting and snorting over the wind. The lights of the ute came around the bend and stopped.

'Are you there, Bid?'

'Yes, Dad, over here. We're coming home. I think I've got them all.'

The men counted the cattle into the paddock as they walked through the headlights. 'Yep, all twenty-six of them. You've done well, mate,' said Biddy's dad.

'Yeah,' said Marty Reed. 'What a cowgirl.'

Biddy took off Bella's bridle and smiled as the pony rubbed gently against her back. It felt good to be a cowgirl.

'We're going to have to let her come with us this year, Lorna. She was pretty handy last night. She did as good a job as anyone, getting those cattle back.'

Biddy's ears pricked up as she sat on the back porch cleaning her school shoes. She didn't have any brothers or sisters, so she shared most of her parents' conversations, but she was also a skilled eavesdropper. She breathed quietly so as not to miss a word.

'I don't know, Dave.' Her mother's voice was doubtful. 'It's a tiring trip. And it's flat out. You know how hard we have to work in some of those rugged places. I won't have time to be looking after her.'

'You won't have to, I'll guarantee.'

Biddy grinned to herself. Good on you, Dad.

'She's as useful as any of the men I could take. Anyway, I was her age when I started going down for the musters.'

'Well, I think—'

The crackle of the radio drowned out the conversation. Grandpa was listening to the morning news.

3

The secret

Biddy walked from the bus stop to her classroom. She felt as if she was buzzing inside. 'I'm going! I'm going! I'm going mustering!' she wanted to yell out.

The noise and babble of the schoolyard seemed distant and irrelevant.

'Hi, Biddy!' It was Irene. Fantastic, she was the one friend Biddy wanted to tell.

'Rene, something good's happening. I shouldn't tell you in case it doesn't work out, but—'

'What? What? Tell me, you rat!'

'Well, I heard Mum and Dad talking this morning and I think they're going to let me go on the muster next week!'

'*Wheee hooo!*' Irene whooped like a rodeo rider. 'Oh, you lucky thing! I've always wanted to go. Dad and Pops tell those old stories about the headland all the time and it sounds so good. The whalebones and the box of bananas, and the dead body, and the wild dogs—'

'And the kangaroo in Alf Brodrick's boat—'

'And the lost man and the human diviner.'

'Yeah, well, I shouldn't get too excited, I guess, 'cause they haven't actually told me I'm going . . . but I can't stop thinking about it.'

'Mmnn . . . ' said Irene, 'it would be up your bum for eavesdropping if you didn't go.'

'Don't,' said Biddy. 'Don't even think about it.'

At lunch time the schoolyard filled with the swish swish of skipping ropes and the chants that went with them. The players lined up and ran in, one by one, while a girl at each end turned the rope over and over. Today there were eleven skippers jumping over the rope in unison. They were going for a school record.

'*Cinderella, dressed in yella, went upstairs to kiss a fella, on the way her panties busted, how many people were disgusted? One, two, three, four . . . '* The girls held each other and jumped as the rope thudded against the asphalt; swish, jump, swish, jump, ' *. . . sixty-five, sixty-six—'*

'Jeez, Biddy! You stepped on the rope!' Sandy Stevens

was wild. 'We were only three off the record!'

'Come on,' said Irene, taking her hand. 'Jenny and Louise can take our places. I want to tell you something.'

Together they wandered down past the monkey bars and sat on the old concrete pipes under the pine trees.

'Remember when we used to wriggle through them, and the time you got stuck in that one, Biddy?'

'Yeah and *you*, my best friend, left me there when the bell rang. It was in grade two, because Mrs Clark had to come down and pull me out. I don't reckon we'd fit now. Anyway, what are you going to tell me?'

Biddy knew that Irene's family, the Rivers, had a secret that was something to do with the headland. It made her nervous. If Irene decided to share it with her, it was serious. No laughing or stupid questions or blabbing to anyone. Ever.

'Hey, I'll braid you while you tell me, if you like.' She sat behind Irene and divided her thick black hair into three bunches. Irene's hair was as black and curly as Biddy's was blonde and straight. When they were little girls they reckoned that if they were horses, Irene would be an Arabian—dark, fine-boned and elegant—and

Biddy would be a palomino quarter horse—chunky and blonde.

'I had an aunty once, and a baby cousin, and they disappeared. Has your mum ever said anything about it to you?'

'No, but I've heard her and Dad talking...'

'That'd be right, Big Ears.'

'She was Joycie, wasn't she?'

'Yep. It's her baby's birthday today. Dad was talking about it at breakfast. He'd have been nine today, just a bit younger than me. People say Joycie was crazy, but Dad says she wasn't. She was just different. She could do anything with horses or cattle, and when she was a kid she rescued a bloke who got lost on Mount Terrible. Everyone else went off looking in the swamp, but Joycie took the dogs the other way and they picked up his scent. She and Dad lived out on the headland when they were kids. Pops, that's my grandfather, was the ranger. He looked after things and serviced the lighthouse. Joycie and Dad didn't go to school. Pops taught them to read and write and do their sums, and the rest of the time they just roamed the headland. Dad reckons there's hardly anywhere they didn't go. They knew all the birds

and animals, the plants, creeks and beaches.'

'Wouldn't it have been fantastic?' Biddy's eyes lit up. 'That's how our fathers met, Rene. Dad and Grandpa always camped at your Pop's when they went down there with the cattle. I heard Dad talking once about how he and Joycie and your dad nicked off one time with the dogs and got into trouble.'

'Yeah, that's right. But stop interrupting. Well, when Dad got old enough for high school, the teachers kicked up a stink and Pops had to move closer to the town. So the kids could have a proper education. Dad reckons all he learned was how to fight. It was the year the war ended, and they closed the ranger's station for a while, so they couldn't have stayed anyway.'

'Their mother died when they were tiny kids, didn't she?' asked Biddy. 'She would have been your grand-mother.'

'Yes. She got bitten by a tiger snake. They got her up to the hospital, but it was too late. Dad reckons that's what made Joycie so strange. It was as if she had no trust. If her mum could just die like that—well, anything could happen. Anyway, Joycie hated school. She just wanted to go back to the headland. That was her place. The town was too hard for her. You know how there's always someone bitching about what someone said about someone else. She couldn't understand that at all. And the townies couldn't cope with her. She was wild. Mad hair, raggy clothes. She was always up a tree or down a rabbit hole. When they made her stay in school she used to cry all day. She didn't make any noise, Dad said, just sat looking out the window with big tears rolling down her face.'

Irene had big tears in her own eyes. Biddy passed her hanky, with the lunch-money change tied in one corner. 'Use the other end,' she said, 'but keep going.'

'She got a boyfriend when she was real young, only about sixteen. Ron Byrnes was a softie, too, and people said they were right for each other; both a bit loopy. Then, as Dad said, surprise, surprise, one thing led to another and Joycie was going to have a baby. They got married and lived in that house down near the sale-yards. The little green one.

'They didn't mix much because most people thought Joycie was weird. Once she went into the hardware store on the way home from going round the traps, and her rabbits bled all over Mrs Hodgin's seed catalogues. Another time the baker said she stole some cake or something, but Dad said she never would have. She was really honest. Ron worked at the mill, and Pops helped them, and when little Joe was born it looked like things were going to work out. And then what happened was crazy.'

'It was a fight at the pub, wasn't it?' asked Biddy.

'No, that's what everyone says, and it makes Ron sound like a drunk. But he didn't drink at the pub, he didn't drink at all. Someone's cattle had got out of the yards and he went down to tell the bloke, that's all. He was doing a good turn. He walked in the pub and straight into a fight. Some mad bugger turned around and belted him, and he hit his head on the floor. It was a fluke. He died right there.'

'Who did it? Did they go to jail?'

'For a while, but it was only manslaughter. You don't go to jail forever for that. Because you didn't really mean to do it. It wasn't a local, just some bloke passing through. Joycie was like a zombie, Dad said. He had to hold her up at the funeral. She couldn't walk. He and Mum got Joycie's stuff and shifted her and the baby in with us and Pops. I was just a toddler. Then one morning, about six months after Ron was killed, they got up and Joycie and Joe were gone.

'They found Pop's old ute down at the jetty, and Thompson's dinghy was missing. They guessed she was going back to the headland, but the easterly blew up that night and the sea was so rough that none of the boats could get out to search. The dinghy showed up the day after, floating upside down near the entrance.'

'And they never found them?' asked Biddy, sniffing.

'No, they were gone. The oars and bits of gear washed up on the beaches, but no one ever saw Joycie or her baby again. They searched all along the coast for tracks in case they got ashore, and Dad and Pops rode over the headland for weeks, looking in all the old places, but they were gone.'

'Irene, that's the saddest story.'

'Yeah, it is sad, but I don't believe the end. I don't reckon they drowned.'

4

Grandpa's story

Biddy peeped into the study from the darkened passage. She could see her grandfather dozing on the couch, with Tigger stretched out on him, blissfully pedalling into his thick woollen jumper. The fire reflected in the old man's reading glasses sitting crookedly on his craggy face, and bathed everything with a warm glow.

Biddy padded into the room in her socks and stood silently, soaking it up. Grandpa was so old. He'd always been here, in this house, ever since she was a baby. She couldn't imagine what it would be like when he was gone. She couldn't bring herself to even think the words 'when he died'.

The room smelt of pipe tobacco, leather, musty books, eucalyptus oil and Grandpa's own special smell. She always thought he smelt like hay.

The pine walls of the room were covered with a

clutter of shelves, paintings and photographs. Biddy knew them all: the horses, the prize bulls, friends in uniform, poems, newspaper clippings, and calendars from years ago with bullock prices scribbled in the margins. There was a series of photographs of her father, faded brown, from when he was a baby to when he was a young man, and he was always on a horse—a series of horses, getting progressively bigger.

The photographs of Biddy were the same. The earliest ones showed her perched on a cushion, on the pommel of her father's saddle, just a squishy baby, with his arm holding her steady. It was as though she'd been born on a horse, her mother used to say. Biddy couldn't remember a time without horses.

Above the fire was her favourite thing in the whole house—a bronze sculpture of a horse galloping out of the sea. The artist had made the waves leap up at its legs like wild dogs and the horse was terrified. Every muscle rippled, and its mane flew back like a banner.

Biddy loved to run her fingers along its fine lines, and the bronze glinted through the tarnish where she had rubbed.

'Come on, boy, keep going, you can do it,' she whispered to the horse.

'What's that?' muttered Grandpa, stirring. 'Oh, it's just you having a word to old dog meat there.'

'Don't call him that, Pa. I reckon he'll get away. Don't you think? Look, he's only got to take another stride and he'll be out onto the hard sand. I wish we knew . . . '

'Mmnn . . . if your grandmother was still alive she'd be able to tell you about it. She brought it back from one of her shopping trips. Picked it up somewhere. Anyway, come over here where I can get a good look at you. My eyes are pretty useless these days.'

Biddy perched on the edge of the couch. 'Dad says you can still see a cow having trouble calving down in the bottom paddock all right.'

'Ho, does he now? That's not how well I can *see*, though. That's knowing what to look for. Being observant. You'll be handy at it, noticing what's going on, if you keep your head on your shoulders. Anyway, what sort of a day have you had?'

'Well . . . Irene and me were talking about the headland at school today. Do you reckon Mum and Dad will let me go this year?'

'Go where?'

'Oh, don't pretend! You know. Go on the muster. Do you reckon they will?'

The old man smiled and stroked the ginger cat lying on his chest. 'This cat would be almost perfect if he didn't dribble when he was happy.'

'Purrrrfect you mean, ha ha. Anyway, what do you reckon?'

He patted her back gently with his misshapen hands. 'Well, I hear you did a pretty good job getting those cows back last night. I reckon you'll go, mate. It's a shame I'm too crook to go with you. We'd be a good team.'

'Oh, Grandpa, I'll remember everything for you. I'll have a story for you for a change. Will you tell me one now? Will you? Tell me *my* story, the one about Biddy's Camp. Then I'll go to bed.'

'All right, dreamer, snuggle in.'

Biddy curled into Grandpa's side, resting her head on his bony shoulder, and patted the purring cat.

'Well, you know you're named after another Biddy, from the early days down here. That Biddy was a convict in Tasmania. Those poor beggars had it terrible hard, you know. Half the time they'd only pinched a few crusts and ended up getting thrown on a ship and transported from England.

'She and some other convicts escaped, stole a whale boat, and rowed all the way across the strait to the mainland, to here. It would have been a wild trip; the sea boils like a cauldron out there. And they wouldn't have been sailors, just ordinary people. None of them would have known how to swim. Anyway, they got across all right but the boat was wrecked on the eastern tip of the headland.

'Biddy was the only survivor. She lived out there by herself, in a bit of a cave at the base of Mount Shadow. It wouldn't have kept much of the weather out. She ate what she could find: shellfish, berries, fish, insects, grubs—'

'Aw cack, Grandpa, that's not true. She didn't eat grubs!'

'My oath she ate grubs. If you're hungry you eat what you find. Anyway, it's all good tucker. It's just different from what you're used to. Where was I? Yes, she lived out there for nearly a year until the Mason brothers found her. They had a huge cattle run, back then, that stretched from the other side of where the town is now to the headland. They were out there looking for strays and they must've got a hell of a fright when she popped up behind a rock. She was terrified. As I said, those convicts were treated pretty bad, especially the women, but the Masons were good, decent fellers.

'They took her back to their homestead. It used to be out on the big plain, but was burnt down when your father was little. The only things left are the old oak trees they planted.'

Biddy nodded. 'I know that place.'

'Well, she stayed there as a cook, and the Masons eventually got her a pardon from the Governor, but she never went back to England. She stayed there at the homestead until she died, an old lady. Your mum reckoned that if you had half her guts you'd be all right, so that's why she called you Biddy.'

5

Joycie's valley

The valley was short and narrow, almost a gully, except for its flat, mossy bottom. At the southern end a waterfall, fringed by coral ferns, trickled down a huge rock face. Over time it had worn away the granite below and made a smooth hollow, like a bath. In the first summer months Joycie often lay there with her baby and let the water wash over them.

The pool overflowed into a stream which meandered through the valley before disappearing into a towering thicket of swordgrass and reeds. This was the creek that Joycie had wriggled up as a little girl, pushing against the current and reeds with the determination of a salmon swimming upstream. It was as though she'd been driven by some need to burrow, to seek shelter. If she hadn't been so small, she'd never have found the valley.

A few steps above the pool a rock platform ran to the base of the cliff where a narrow fissure led to Joycie's cave. She had found this cave as a child, and she had imagined the fine home it would make ... the bed here, the fire there, under the crevice that opened up to the sky. That had been play; a small girl's fantasy. Now she was actually living here, and her secret valley was as good as she had imagined.

The valley ran north, so it was always flooded with light. It nestled between two jagged ranges, so choked with fallen timber that Joycie didn't think anyone would ever climb them and look down into her valley. Even if they did, she thought, all they would see would be treetops.

Although Joycie had done something crazy, she had been clever enough to do it well. She wanted everyone to believe that she and her baby had drowned, so she could be alone, truly alone, until her head cleared and she was strong again. When she pushed the boat out into the current, that night she disappeared, she had left extra bags of supplies in it. It would have looked too suspicious if none of her gear washed up. In her other bags, the bags she kept, were the things she knew she could not survive without. She took a tomahawk, two blankets, an oilskin coat, a cast-iron cooking pot, some water containers, a cigarette lighter, her mother's sewing box, a good knife and sharpening stone, pencils, paper, her little .22 rifle, ammunition, a couple of rabbit traps and books. Books had always been her escape from the real world, and she could not have lived without them, or her comics. Joycie loved *Phantom* comics. She took a bundle with her, stored carefully in a watertight tin.

The days were full. Joycie was kept busy finding and cooking food. When Joe was little she did everything with him on her hip.

Sphagnum moss was perfect for lining the baby's nappies, dry ferns and seaweed made a comfortable bed underneath their blankets, and the rabbits Joycie trapped provided furs and meat. She could never bring herself to shoot kangaroos and wallabies because their faces were so sweet. She didn't need to anyway; the fish and shellfish in the bay were so easy to get that they always had plenty to eat. Joycie roasted the seeds of kangaroo grass and saltbush, and she'd brought silverbeet and rhubarb plants with her. Her dad used to say that if you had them in the garden, you always had a meal. Joycie planted them next to the stream, kept the soil fertilised with seaweed and rabbit droppings, and they grew like weeds.

The headland was shaped like a boot, with the bay at the top, the wild surf beach to the west, and a series of bays on the east, separated by rocky points. A broken chain of mountains ran through the middle, surrounded by an untidy patchwork of swamps, plains, sand dunes, forests and valleys.

The ranger lived on the west coast, and that was where the drovers travelled, so Joycie didn't go there much. She found a way to climb out of the valley so she could get to the eastern beaches, and this was her most used track. She dragged driftwood back to their camp and fitted it together to make a table, a bench, seats and a wooden horse.

One winter a sperm whale washed ashore, and months later, when its flesh had rotted away, Joycie made trip after trip to carry the giant vertebrae home. She sat them in a long line beside the stream, and one of Joe's favourite games was to jump from one to the other without touching the ground.

'You're running along a whale!' Joycie called to him. 'Look! Right along its spine.' She guided his fingers so he could feel his own vertebrae; the same, but so much smaller.

Over the years the valley became as decorated as a bowerbird's nest. When Joe began to walk, he toddled along the beach behind her. They played in the golden sand, and they were in the sea so often that Joe swam like a little seal before he was two. They explored the crystal clear pools scattered amongst the rocks like jewel boxes, filled with anemones, starfish, crabs and bubble weed. Each day the sea washed up something

new. She threaded the treasures they found onto fishing line, and made spider webs of sea-urchins, starfish, sea-dragons and shells which danced from the trees around their home.

Joycie made a swing for Joe from washed-up rope and driftwood, and she turned an old fishing net into a fine hammock—under the shady blackwood in summer, and strung beside the cave-fire in winter. She had to do something, make something, every day, or she felt the heebie-jeebies creeping up on her.

Winter was the hardest time, especially when Joe was tiny and it was too cold and wet to take him outside. Then, sometimes, they stayed in the cave for days, drawing, reading, keeping the fire going. Once she'd done her work she could relax, and then she and Joe would lie in the hammock, playing and singing together. She played his favourite tunes on the old mouth organ, tapping out the time with her foot, smiling as he sang and danced around on his chubby legs. She loved the bush, and although the sadness in her heart did not fade, she was quiet and restful, compared to the jumpy way she felt in town.

Ron was on her mind a hundred times a day. The little

time they had together seemed like a dream now. She had a photograph in a silver frame of them on their wedding day, looking so happy; a lifetime ahead of them. So they thought.

She missed her brother and dad, too. She still talked aloud to them. She didn't realise just how much she talked until one day she heard Joe murmuring as he played in the sand, 'Sorry Mick, sorry Dad.' Over and over in his baby sing-song voice, 'Sorry Mick, sorry Dad.'

Joycie didn't have a calendar to count the days but she put a charcoal mark on the wall of her cave every year when the purple flags started to flower. The day Joe was born she had looked out the hospital window and noticed a clump of them blooming, so that was how she remembered his birthday. She knew the date, October the fifth, but she had no way of telling exactly when it was; she just knew that when the purple flags flowered it was time to celebrate Joe's birthday. Joycie was shocked to realise one day that there were eight marks on the wall.

She felt very close to her mother on the headland. In the blue-and-silver tin, in a box, safe in the cave, was a photograph of her cradling baby Joyce and smiling stiffly for the camera. Joycie knew her smile wouldn't really have been like that. It was just the way a photograph made you feel: all shy to be looked at so hard. She had such a tender face, with soft olive skin and crinkly black hair.

Another photograph was of her brother Mick, and her father, both on horses, squinting into the sun. They sat easily, with their feet forward, stockwhips looped over their shoulders, ready for anything. Joycie's heart always skipped a beat when she thought of them. It was a terrible thing she had done. She promised herself she'd go back, explain to them, ease their pain. But it was always too hard. She'd tell herself they were tough, they were men; her father had kept going when their mum had died, hadn't he? But it nagged at her. Nagged like the pain that had been poking at her for nearly two years now.

When it first happened, she thought she'd eaten too many rock oysters. The next time, the native cherries were to blame. But the last pain had brought her to her knees when it hit, and put her into a dead sweat. For the first time she thought she really might have to go back.

When she came to live at the valley, all those years ago, her biggest fear had been that Joe would get seriously sick; sick in a way that she couldn't fix with tea-tree oil or a cool cloth. But he never had. He was always well. And now her body was letting her down. Joe couldn't care for her if she got really sick. He was only eight. He was too little to be on his own.

When she thought like this, she would take out her mother's shell necklace from the tin. The necklace came from Seal Island, her father had told her, beyond the headland. It was made from hundreds of tiny shells, each a luminous green, and shone as though it had an energy of its own. Even in the faded sepia portrait of her mother it seemed to glow at her throat. It was Joycie's most treasured thing.

6

Living in the bush

Joycie and Joe rose with the sun and went to bed at nightfall. As Joe grew older they had more and more fun together, spearing fish in the shallow lake, body surfing out at the ocean beach, laughing at the old echidna who trundled into their valley. He was always so intent on finding ants that he'd come right up to them if they lay very still in his path. Once Joycie grabbed him with her jumper, so his spikes didn't stick in, and they turned him over and pulled the ticks off his furry tummy. His fur was like brown velvet, so soft you could hardly feel it, and he was as shy as a timid child, covering his face with his little clawed hands.

Their valley was filled with birds. They had no fear of Joycie and Joe, and flitted and perched all around them: wrens, parrots, warblers, and their favourite, the grey thrush. The only time they would dart for cover was when the shadow of a hawk or eagle crossed the valley floor. Joe could mimic all their songs, and knew their nests and where they built them. He and Joycie collected feathers and jammed them into cracks around the cave. Joe would lie in bed at night and watch them quivering in the draft from the fire.

Joycie showed Joe piles of mussel shells left by the people who'd lived on the headland for thousands of years. 'You know those dingoes we hear sometimes at night?' she asked. 'That howling? Well, their ancestors would have belonged to those people. They would have been the women's dogs. When the people were driven away, the dogs became wild.'

Joe liked to think of people living on the headland, just like him and Joycie.

They fished mainly on the rugged eastern coast of the headland, where they were less likely to be seen. Not that there was anyone much to see them. They sometimes saw cattle on the flats behind the ocean beach, and occasionally boats came ashore for water from their little creek. Joycie collected dingo droppings and scattered them through the swordgrass there, to put the fishermen's dogs off the scent.

Once they were nearly discovered by a group of men and women who came so silently through the sand dunes that Joycie and Joe had to race into the scrub like the wind, leaving their oysters unshelled on the beach. The people camped at Middle Spring for a week, walking every day to different places collecting flowers and taking photographs.

One day Joe crept into their camp while they were out exploring and did some investigating of his own. He reached into the tiny tents and gasped at the softness of their sleeping bags. He searched through the food, gorging himself on chocolate and spitting out the bitter

coffee he tasted. As he left, he brushed away his footprints with a branch, and his visit would have stayed a
secret but for the beautiful red knife that fell out of his
shirt as Joycie tucked him into bed that night. She had
told him not to touch any of their things, to stay away,
and she felt sick when she saw the Swiss Army knife.
She smacked him, the only time she ever did, and told
him terrible stories about what the people would do to
little boys they found snooping in their camp. Then she
took the knife and rushed out into the night, leaving him
sobbing and confused at the way she'd turned on him.

But when he woke the next morning, she was laughing.
'I crept up to their camp and they were talking about the
knife. See, you naughty boy, they already missed it. You
can't take people's things. I sat and waited until they
went to bed and then I tossed the knife, a big high toss,
and it landed right in the middle of all the tents. I was
about to leave when, suddenly, out of one tent pops a
head, staring at the knife lying there in the firelight. He
must of heard it land. The man crawled out and picked
up the knife and he scratched his head. He just kept
scratching his head!'

Joe kept his distance after that, but he could see they were gentle people. They seemed to care about this place of his and the animals and plants that lived in it, and he really couldn't believe the stories Joycie told.

It was the same with the drovers. When they brought the cattle down, or came to muster, Joycie tried to keep him in the valley, and told him what bad people they were. But as he grew older, Joe could see this wasn't true.

In fact, Joycie knew who the drovers were. It would be the Frasers. She used to muck around with Dave Fraser when she was a kid. But she wasn't going to tell Joe that. Dave was probably just like the rest now.

Joe was used to the cattle—they were around all winter—and they were fun to chase, if Joycie didn't see. But the horses, Joe loved the horses—their manes, their swishing tails, and the gentle nickering that greeted him when he crept up to pat them in the night. The last time the drovers came, Joe defied Joycie and shadowed the cattle and horses for two days until they left. He wasn't game to let himself be seen, but at night he lay in the dark like a hungry dog, devouring the scraps of stories and songs that drifted from the campfire. He went back to the valley determined to make Joycie see that she was wrong, that these people would not hurt him, but she was so distraught, so crazy with worry that he couldn't begin to explain. When she finally calmed down, she held him fiercely and wept into his hair. 'I thought you'd gone. I thought they'd taken you.' Her voice was thick against his neck. 'You think they look like nice people but I know. I've been in the town. Never, never let anyone see you. They'll take you away. They killed your dad. Even Pops couldn't save him.'

Joe sighed and hugged her close. It wasn't Joycie looking after him any more. It was him looking after Joycie.

That night they sat on the whale rock that jutted into the sea at Whiting Beach. Joycie hummed a tune but Joe didn't join in. His mind was racing. Joycie's fear made him wary, and he was bound to stay and care for her, but the lights across the bay were drawing him like a moth to a flame.

7

The muster

The stars were still bright in the night sky. Biddy sat on her pony at the garden fence, waiting impatiently to begin the ride down to the headland. She had never been up so early, let alone in the saddle at this hour. The biting wind was waking her, but the porridge she'd eaten for breakfast, and her woolly gloves and beanie and new oilskin coat, kept her snug and warm.

Bella wasn't used to being saddled so early. She stamped and jiggled, her silver mane glinting in the light from the house.

'I wish you were coming,' Biddy called to her grandfather.

He looked so old and skinny waving from the back porch, with Tigger weaving around his legs. She hoped he'd be okay. Still, they'd only be gone for a night. They'd be back with the cattle by Thursday evening.

'An old bloke like me would only get in your way. My word, you're a flash-looking outfit. Do your oilskin up. It'll be freezing out on the beach.'

'Righto, let's get a move on.' Biddy's dad tightened a final strap on Blue, the packhorse, then swung into his saddle. His old stockhorse, Gordon, stood quietly. He was a great horse, willing and intelligent. Once, years ago, Dad had ridden him into a marshy place, looking for cattle, and nearly got bogged, but Gordon had escaped by testing the ground with his hoof, one step at a time, until he was sure it would hold his weight.

'We'll see you pretty late tomorrow. Don't forget to leave the gate open into the yard paddock—'

'Of course I'll leave the gate open!' Grandpa had never got used to his son telling him what to do. 'Don't *you* forget to look in behind Mount Smoky. There's always a few stragglers in there. And look out for the quicksand!'

'Yeah, we will. Bye, Dad.'

'Look after yourself, Dad,' called Biddy's mum as she gathered her reins. 'Take care.'

They turned their horses and rode away in the early morning dark, with the packhorse and dogs trotting behind. Biddy kept twisting in her saddle and calling back to the figure in the doorway, 'Bye, Grandpa. Look after Tigger for me. Bye, Grandpa. Love you,' until they crested the low hill beyond the stockyards, and the house was blocked from view.

They were three tiny figures riding over the plain. The headland was a vague shape to the south, and to the east the water of the bay lay flat and grey. Biddy and her parents were riding west to the shallow inlet behind their farm. They would follow the bridle path over the cliffs to the surf beach, which was the only way of getting to the headland. There was no road, and the mudflats on the bay were impassable.

Biddy thought there couldn't be a better feeling than riding off into unknown country, on a good horse, with who knows what adventure ahead. It was like being an explorer, or an outlaw. She wished she had a revolver. It would be great to take potshots at rabbits as you galloped along.

The sky was just light enough for the horses to pick their way along the track. They trotted, fresh and skittish at first, then settled into a steady rhythm. The saddle-bags on the packhorse bounced in time to the hoofbeats.

By the time they got through the scrub and out onto the cliff tops, the sky in the east was blazing pink and orange. 'Hey, Mum!' yelled Biddy. 'Pink sky in the morning, shepherd's warning! Means it's going to rain.'

She held on tight and tried not to look down. They only used this path when the tide was in, as it was now. It was too narrow to drive cattle along; they'd push past each other and fall down the cliff. Biddy looked at the water surging below her, and shivered. When they came back with the cattle the tide would be out and they'd ride on the sand.

The path wound over the last cliff, then dropped steeply to the surf beach. Biddy leaned back, and Bella slid down the sandy slope on her hindquarters. Ah! It felt good to be back on flat ground.

Far out to sea the sunlight sparkled on the water like sequins. Sullen clouds hung over the peaks of the headland. The beach was long, endless. It ran for miles, then disappeared into the sea-mist. The dunes towered on one side and the surf pounded in on the other. A freezing wind whipped straight up from Antarctica, blasting sand and rain into their faces. The high tide forced them to ride along the base of the dunes, in soft sand littered with driftwood and seaweed thrown up by the violent waves. Biddy skittered about on her pony, looking for treasures. She peered closely at any bottles, in case there was a message inside.

Once, in the old days, Grandpa had found a crate of bananas. Bananas were a luxury back then, he told Biddy, so they'd had a big feed of them, and packed the rest in their saddlebags. They hadn't gone much further down the beach when they found another box, about the same size as the first. More bananas, they thought, and whipped the lid off—only to find a dead body inside. Some poor soul had been buried at sea, and washed ashore. Grandpa said he never ate bananas after that, but Biddy was sure she'd seen him.

Her parents rode together in an easy silence, their horses striding out, heads down into the wind and squalling rain. Sooty oyster-catchers and sandpipers darted along the waterline, and crying seagulls, chased by the dogs, wheeled overhead.

8

Calling the cattle

It took all morning to ride along the beach, and it was a relief to get out of the howling wind and into the shelter of the bush when they reached Brandy Creek. The rain had stopped and they laid their oilskin coats out on the mossy bank and had lunch. Biddy was tired already, but she wouldn't dare let her parents know that. A thin bit of sun crept through the cloud, and the small fire her mother made to boil the billy warmed her. Corned beef sandwiches, hot sweet black tea in a chipped enamel mug, and a slab of fruitcake filled her up. She'd never drink black tea at home, but it seemed just the thing here in the bush. The three of them snuggled together like a family of lions and snoozed until Mum's dog, Top, woke them, trying to get into the food bag.

'Get out of it, you mongrel of a thing,' growled Biddy. 'That's our food.'

'Hey, Bid,' her mother teased, 'imagine if he ate all our food and we had to live on witchetty grubs until we got home!'

'Like the Biddy I'm named after. She lived out here and survived on what she could find. Grandpa told me.'

They rode through the lightly timbered gullies that afternoon, calling to the cattle and putting out little piles of salt for them. These cattle had been bred up in the high country and were used to coming out of the bush to get the salt they craved so much.

Biddy was the salt girl. She waited on Bella in a clearing, with the heavy bag of salt on the pommel of her saddle. She called to the cattle, 'Saaalt! Saaalt!' over and over.

Slowly the steers trickled down the gullies and ridges. They were wary at first, because they hadn't seen a horse and rider for months, but they soon settled to lick the salt from the ground. Biddy rode around the edge of the mob, keeping the cattle together and soothing them with her voice.

Her parents had taken the dogs and headed in opposite directions to search some of the remote places that they knew the cattle loved. Mum took Top, because he wouldn't work for Dad, and Dad took Nugget, because he wouldn't work for Mum. Neither of the dogs worked for Biddy, which made her really mad. It was as if they didn't think she knew how things should be done. She could whistle and yell until she was blue in the face and they'd just give her a sly doggy smile and keep on doing what they were doing.

Biddy hoped her parents wouldn't take too long to get back with the other cattle. The mob was a bit jumpy. The steers kept looking at old Blue, the packhorse, who was tethered beside a thick mass of paperbarks and sword-grass. It was as if they thought he had two heads and was going to attack them. Biddy couldn't see what was so scary about Blue. He was just standing there, half asleep, resting one back leg. But the cattle continued to snort and stare at him.

Finally, way off in the distance, she heard stockwhips cracking and dogs barking. Good, either Mum or Dad would be back soon, and then if the cattle stampeded it wouldn't be her fault. Soon Lorna appeared through the scrub, pushing a ragged group of steers towards them.

The cattle bellowed out to each other. As the mobs mingled together, Biddy told her mother about the cattle spooking at Blue.

'They wouldn't be spooking at him,' she answered, crossing one leg over the pommel of her saddle and giving her horse, Dusky, a pat. 'Phew! It's hard work getting cattle out of those gullies. The scrub is so thick you wouldn't know what was in there. But I love this mare. She'll barge her way through anything.'

'If they're not spooking at him,' said Biddy, 'what are they afraid of?'

'It must be something in that bush behind him, I guess.'

'Then why isn't Blue spooking at it too?' Biddy persisted.

'Mmmn,' Mum thought for a while. 'Perhaps it's something he's not afraid of.'

Dad came into the clearing soon after with more cattle. His horse, Gordon, dripping with sweat, had foam on his neck where the reins had rubbed, and his nostrils flared red. He reminded Biddy of Grandpa's bronze horse, all wet and shining.

Some of the bullocks were huge, with long curved horns. They stared, wild-eyed, and made half charges at the horses before huddling together in the centre of the mob.

'The old man was right!' Dad called to them. 'These eight crazy ones were around the back of Mount Smoky. They've been there for two years by the look of their horns. Watch it, Biddy. If they come near you, get out of the way.'

'Yes, Bid, they could really hurt you,' said Mum. 'But they'll be worth a fortune if we can get them to market. Well done, Dave.'

It took the rest of the afternoon to drive the cattle back to the holding yards. The yards had been built a long time ago, by felling trees to form a barricade. Over the years drovers had added more and more branches to make a tangle of wood that even the wildest bullock couldn't get through.

Mum counted the mob into the yard. 'One hundred and seventy-five,' she told Biddy and Dad as they tied up the sliprails. 'Counting that extra eight you got, there's still thirty-three to find. Tomorrow morning we'll go back to some of the places we left salt and see what we can pick up. We've done well, team.'

Biddy couldn't move. She sat on a patch of the softest, bright green moss, pushing it down with her fingers and watching it spring up again. A smooth granite boulder supported her back, and her woolly clothes and oilskin coat still kept her warm. Only her feet were cold, frozen in boots that had got wet early and never dried out. A yellow-breasted robin flitted down from the tea-tree, through the last rays of sun that made the wattles glow. It was a golden world.

Long shadows ran across to where her parents were rubbing down the horses. She had started to groom Bella, but was so impatient and bad tempered with fatigue that her mother sent her to sit and rest. Dad would start a fire soon, and after tea they'd roll out their swags and sleep beside it. Even the wild cattle had settled in the yard, and the dogs slept, bone weary, beside the packhorse. They knew where their dinner was.

'You thieving mongrel! That rotten dog's stolen our bacon!' Biddy woke to her father's angry shouts, and she felt cheesed-off too. She'd been really looking forward to eggs and bacon for breakfast. She didn't think Top could have stolen anything, though. He'd been in her swag all night, but she wasn't going to tell her mother that. Lorna would be very grumpy to know a flea-bag dog had slept in Biddy's swag. She gave a kick to dislodge him, and hauled on his collar. 'Sorry, mate, you're in trouble. Better you than me, though. Thanks for being such a good foot-warmer.'

Even without the bacon, it was a good breakfast. Biddy toasted the bread on a long twisted-wire fork, and her father fried up eggs in the pan.

Mum came back from saddling the horses. 'Yoohoo! This smells good enough to eat! Oh, you *are* eating it.'

'Very funny, Mum. Yours is there next to the fire,' said Biddy. 'How are the horses this morning?'

'Good, mmmnn, good. I like the way you've plaited their manes. Very fancy. Did Irene teach you that?'

Biddy screwed up her nose. 'What plaits? I haven't been plaiting them. Ask Dad. I just got up.'

9

The store

Joycie knew how to live off the land, but she and Joe would have had a lean time without their extra supplies. As long as Joycie could remember, Mad Dan had lived at the southern end of the headland. He was an old hermit, terrified of people, who'd built a shack for himself years ago. When Joycie and her brother were little kids they made up a song about him—*Dan Dan the dirty man, washed his face in a frying pan*—and their father had sent them to bed hungry for being so mean.

Pops was one of the few who had ever seen him, and when he was the ranger he always left the storeroom unlocked for the old fellow to help himself to supplies. Nobody ever talked about it, even now, but everyone knew that part of the ranger's job was to leave the store open for Dan. That was how the system worked.

Joycie just helped herself from the same store. When

Joe was a baby and she had to carry him all day to get there, it was hard, but later it became good fun. 'Wanna go to the store, Jozz?' Joe would say. 'There's no sugar left.'

It was where they got their clothes from, too. When Joycie had fled the town, she'd packed some toddler's clothes for Joe, but nothing bigger. She never dreamed they'd be on their own for all these years, so as he grew she had to cut down and alter shirts and trousers of her own to fit him. They looked funny but they were comfortable and warm.

Joycie lined their jackets with rabbit skins and made fur-lined moccasins to wear in the winter. Joe had never worn shoes, and Joycie hadn't for years. Their feet were so calloused and tough they didn't really look like feet; they were more like hooves. When the weather was cold, it was a pleasure to pull on their soft, furry boots.

Over the years Joycie mended and darned and put patches on patches, but eventually their clothes just wore away. The store was the only place they could turn to.

'Poor old Dan,' laughed Joycie as she pulled on a pair of the ranger's work pants. 'They'll reckon he's getting greedy.'

On these visits they'd lie on the hill behind the buildings and watch for a long time to make sure the ranger was away. If his dog was unchained they never went in, and it was a long walk home empty-handed. But if the dog was on the chain it meant the ranger was gone, and they would climb down to collect their supplies. Powdered milk, tea, flour, sugar, matches—nobody seemed to notice that a bit more was disappearing. The first time the dog saw them he went mad, barking like an idiot. After that Joycie always made sure she had a fresh piece of rabbit for him, and he became their friend, fawning and slobbering.

'I'd love a dog,' Joe said one day, looking into his yellow eyes, 'even a dopey one like this.'

Joycie frowned. 'You can't have a dog. It's just you and me, Joe. Just you and me.'

10

In the cave

Outside the cave, wind and rain slashed through the bush. Joe lay in the hammock watching the shadows of the fire flicker across Joycie's face. He was carving a piece of cuttlefish, powdering the soft white shell with his fingers, but with no purpose. His mother was sick. She'd had pains before, but not like this one today. She'd collapsed onto the big driftwood bed this morning and not got up again. All afternoon she'd said how cold and sick she felt, so he'd made a huge fire and put all the rugs and blankets on her, but she still shivered. She'd been asleep for ages, now. Maybe she needed a drink. Her face was so pale.

'Jozz,' he whispered, leaning across from the hammock. She didn't move. 'Jozz! Wake up!' Nothing. He leapt across to her bed and shook her shoulders urgently. 'You have to wake up, Jozzie! Please!' She always woke up for him. She was always there. 'Jozz! Jozz! Can you hear me?'

He put his cheek against her face and felt her soft breath. Good. Maybe she just needed a big sleep. Joe lay beside Joycie on the bed, his arm across her, his face buried in her hair. When I wake up she'll be better, he thought, she'll be better.

When he woke the storm outside was raging, but in the cave it was still and silent. The fire was just a glow, and Joycie lay as she had when he went to sleep. She was cold. He felt for her breath. There was none. He pushed the blankets aside and pressed his ear against her chest, listening for a heartbeat. Nothing. He shifted his head urgently. Sometimes it was hard to hear. Nothing.

'Come on, Jozz. No! You can't be . . . !' He took her hand and rubbed it between his, but her fingers were cool and limp. A choking pain of grief welled in his throat. He knew death. He knew when life was gone.

He knelt beside the bed for a long time with his head against his mother's chest, talking to her, crying, keening. After a while he tidied the bed and tucked the blankets in, pushed the fire together and picked the cup up from the floor; putting things right. Then he realised it was never going to be right. Never going to be the same. He was alone.

Suddenly the cave felt like a tomb, and his mother... well, that wasn't his mother. She was gone. He couldn't stay here without her. He pulled down the big bag and began packing, wildly at first, but then with more consideration. The rabbit-skin rug, the *Phantom* comics, the blue-and-silver tin, clothes, gear, anything he would need for... what? For life? Where was he going?

He carried the bag to the mouth of the cave then turned to look back. A thought struck him, and he felt in his bag for the tin, opened it carefully and took out the Seal Island necklace. He walked back to the bed, gently placed the shells around his mother's face, then pressed his cheek against hers, breathing in the scent of her beautiful hair one last time.

The rain stung his face as he swung his bag onto the platform outside the cave. He felt for the pile of rocks he knew was there. One of Joycie's *Phantom* comics told a tale of giant tigers, and when he was a very little boy he couldn't stop worrying about them. Joycie had laughed and reassured him, but he had insisted on carting rocks up to the cave so if the tigers ever did attack they could barricade themselves inside. The rocks had sat there ever since. Now he packed them carefully in the entrance, stacking them one on top of the other, sealing it so that his mother would not be disturbed.

The rain streamed down his face. He could taste the salt of his tears. His hands were numb with cold. Lightning flashes showed him that the wall was nearly finished. He packed wet earth into the cracks, then rested his head for a moment against the rock wall. He shouldered the bag and made his way across the valley, past the pool, past the swing, past the shells spinning in the wind. The bush lit up, blue and ghostly, as he climbed the track, but he didn't look back.

Ferns and branches lashed him as he picked his way along a roaring creek. The rain beat down. He walked for hours without direction, just going. On and on. He had no idea where he was. Resting for a moment in the lee of a rock, he heard a noise over the racket of the storm. He listened carefully, and yes, there was a crying sound just above him. He left his bag and climbed up the slippery rock, scraping his knees, but hardly feeling it for the cold. He peered into the gloom of a low cave, then the clouds parted to let moonlight in, and he saw a dingo pup, whimpering beside its mother. He crawled under the overhang. The pup bared its teeth and growled at him fiercely, backing behind its mother. She didn't move. Joe put his hand on her and knew that she had been dead for days. She was cold and stiff. Joe sniffed. She smelt bad. He gagged at the thought that this would happen to Joycie, too.

'Here, pup,' Joe crooned. 'Here, pup. We need each other, I reckon.' He grabbed the dingo, ignoring the needle-sharp teeth, and held him close in the folds of his shirt, then wriggled to the edge of the cave where the air was fresher. He looked out into the night, into the rain, and rocked to and fro, talking to the pup all the time. 'There, there, little dog. There, there. You'll be right, mate. You'll be right.' It was the way Joycie used to talk to him when he got scared of the dark. It made him feel better, too. After a while the tiny body began to nestle against him, then a small black nose and two bright eyes peeped out between his buttons.

When the rain finally eased and the moon came out, Joe climbed down the rock, holding the pup close with one arm, picked up his bag, and slipped like a shadow through the bush.

11

Droving along the beach

The cattle splashed between the paperbarks that grew in the shallow tannin-stained river. Massive granite boulders loomed over the stream. They were patched with orange lichen and blackened by centuries of trickling rain. The mountains rose steeply on either side.

Biddy and her parents had rounded up two hundred and three cattle altogether, which meant there were five missing. Perhaps they'd died, or maybe some were tucked away in a far-off gully that hadn't been searched. They'd have to wait until next autumn to find out. Biddy rode on the side of the mob, keeping them headed down the river. The bush above was dense, making the valley hot and ripe with the smell of cattle, sweat and earth.

At the beach the air suddenly freshened. When the cattle saw the wide expanse of sand they broke into a trot. Biddy cantered to wheel them to the right, towards home, and it felt good to be out of the bush at last, out in the open, with the seagulls scattering ahead. The wind had died away and a gentle breeze blew up from the south, pushing fat puffs of cloud through the blue October sky. It was a perfect day.

Once the cattle were all on the beach and had settled into a mob, Biddy reached into her saddlebag and found the sandwiches her mother had made that morning. They wouldn't have time to stop for lunch today. It would be low tide soon, and they would have to keep going to get the mob around the entrance to the inlet while there was still enough room on the beach. Once the tide was right in, the water ran swift and deep against the cliffs. Grandpa had been trapped there years ago with a freak tide, and the thought of cattle drowning in the cold current still gave Biddy the horrors.

It was easy droving along the beach. The sand dunes were as steep as cliffs, so the cattle couldn't drift back into the bush. Biddy's dad rode in the lead, ahead of the mob, steadying any that were inclined to run, and giving the others something to follow. The Wild Ones, as they'd christened the big steers from behind Mount Smoky, were right behind him, heads up and bellowing. Mad barking and whip-cracking told Biddy each time one tried to break past the lead, as her father plied his stock-whip and the dogs headed the beast.

It was almost as though the dogs enjoyed having a few bad cattle; it gave them an excuse to do serious biting. They trotted along before the mob, watching the Wild Ones over their shoulders, as if to say, 'Come on then, do you want another go? Come on, we're ready.' They would be much quieter cattle by the time they got home. 'Educating' was what her father called it, and Biddy thought he enjoyed it as much as the dogs.

Mum rode at the back with the packhorse, pushing along the dawdlers. Biddy was on the seaward side, splashing steadily through the shallows and turning back any steers that wandered towards the surf or stopped to chew on the rubbery yellow kelp washed in with the tide. She rested one leg across the pommel of her saddle and wondered again who really had plaited the horses' manes last night. She was pretty sure her mum and dad weren't tricking her, and the plaits weren't just tangles. Gordon's tail was braided in the same way she and Irene did their hair, and Mum's horse had a running plait sloping down her neck. Bella's mane had three fine single plaits, with speckled feathers bound into the ends of them. Maybe the next time she braided Irene's hair she would try it. She had some crimson rosella feathers that would look fantastic in her black hair. Perhaps some red beads...

'Biddy! Biddy!' Her mother's voice broke into her daydream. 'Go out and get those cattle off the sandbar.'

Without thinking, Biddy clicked Bella into a canter and raced after the long straggle of steers. Bella put her ears back as she wheeled the cattle around, and gave them a dirty look.

'Get back there! Git moving!' Biddy shouted. 'You boys can't even swim!'

Bella's hooves pounded as she raced alongside the galloping steers.

The shifting clouds overhead reflected in the wet sand so that the ground itself seemed to be moving...

12

Quicksand

Later, Biddy tried to remember what happened, but there was no warning, no deep sand, no bog. It was just bang— straight in. One minute Bella was bowling along on firm sand, and the next she had stopped. The sudden halt flung Biddy over the pony's head.

At first she thought Bella had fallen, so she staggered to her feet and urged the pony to do the same. 'Come on, Bella! Come on, girl! Get up!' It was only when she felt the sand sucking at her legs that she realised what had happened.

'Mum!' she screamed. 'Mum! Help me! Bella's bogged! She's in quicksand!' Bella struggled and sank even deeper, past her shoulders. 'Oh please, God, I'll do anything. Please don't let her sink! Come *on*, Bella! Get out!'

Biddy dragged on the reins. Bella grunted with effort and heaved desperately, but couldn't budge. The bridle pulled over the pony's slippery ears and came away in Biddy's hands, sending her sprawling into the bog. She lay there, sandy, wet and sobbing, as her mother rode up and dismounted on the firm sand.

'Come on, Bid. Get up. We'll see if Blue can pull her out.' She looped a rope around the chest of the old pack-horse and threw the end to Biddy. 'Tie this under her surcingle—where it goes across the top of your saddle. If you lie flat on the sand you won't sink so much.'

Biddy wriggled across to Bella. The pony had stopped struggling but it made Biddy sob to see her looking so pathetic. Her beautiful mane was plastered into a brown lump and her terrified eyes were messed and dirty with sand. At least she wasn't sinking any more.

'Don't worry, girl,' Biddy soothed. 'You'll be right.'

The rope was heavy and stiff, and her hands just wouldn't stop shaking. She pulled off her gloves and flung them away. 'I hope this strap will hold, Mum. Okay, you pull and I'll push.'

Lorna turned Blue towards the shore and he leaned into the rope around his chest. He dug his hooves in the sand and heaved with all his might... Suddenly he plunged forward—but without Bella. Only the broken surcingle dragged on the end of the rope.

'It's not working, Mum!' Biddy screamed. 'It's broken! She hasn't shifted!'

Lorna backed up Blue again. She tried to undo the rope from the surcingle, but the knot had pulled tight and hard. She cursed under her breath. She didn't want Biddy to see how desperate she felt. 'I'll have to cut it off, Bid. Hang on a minute.'

She freed the rope with her knife and threw it back. 'We'll try again. This time thread it under your saddle, under the pommel.'

Biddy tied it. She felt so slow, so clumsy. She pushed against Bella's side, but with no strength. She couldn't get any purchase in the slop. 'Come on, Blue, this time. Pull!'

Blue dug his hooves in again and heaved against the rope. He groaned and Bella shifted slightly, but then— again—Blue lurched forward without her. This time the whole saddle dragged on the end of the rope.

'Biddy, darling, I'm sorry, but we're going to have to leave her.'

'*What?*' Biddy struggled out of the quicksand to where her mother was stowing the rope in the pack-saddle.

'You can't leave her! When the tide comes in she'll drown!' Biddy screamed. 'I'll go and get Dad. He'll get her out.' Tears were streaming down her face. She started to run.

'No, Biddy.' Lorna gathered her bedraggled daughter in her arms. 'Stop fighting me. Dad can't come back here. He's got to hold the lead. But even if he did come back, he couldn't do anything. There's nowhere to tie a rope on to now. We can't put a rope around her neck. She'd choke. And her tail's under the sand. Besides, we've got to get these cattle off the beach or we could lose them...' Her voice trailed off.

'You were going to say "too", weren't you? Lose them *too*,' Biddy accused her mother. 'You think she'll *drown* if we leave her. We can't do it.' She stuck out her chin. 'I'll stay.'

'Darling, you can*not* stay.' Lorna pulled dry clothes out of the saddlebag. 'Here, put these on. You are a ten-year-old girl and I can't leave you here alone. Come on, I'll help you out of all that wet stuff, and tell you about Taffy. You know the story. He didn't drown. He came home.'

It was like undressing a doll. Biddy was so stunned and cold that she just stared dumbly at Bella and listened to the story as her mother peeled off the sodden, sandy clothes.

'Taffy was a buckskin horse that Grandpa had when Dad was about your age. He was enormous; wide as well as tall. Your grandma used to say you could eat dinner off his back. I think he might have had one blue eye, but I'm not sure. I only know the story as your dad has told me. He was so quiet and kind that sometimes, just for fun, Dad and Grandma and Grandpa would all ride him together.'

'Triple-dinking,' Biddy said in a flat voice.

'What?'

'Triple-dinking. Like double-dinking, but with three.'

'Oh, yeah.' Lorna was relieved that Biddy was listening, was at least interested in the story. 'Anyway, one day Grandpa was bringing cattle home along the beach. Your dad wasn't with him. He was still too little to go. A man called Steve Begg was helping, riding Taffy, and just like you they got stuck in the quicksand. They had to leave him, just like we're leaving Bella, and Steve rode the packhorse home, just like you're going to ride Blue.

'Well, they got home very late, and your dad and grandmother were terribly upset to hear that Taffy was bogged. They really loved that horse. They sat in the kitchen weeping and remembering what a good horse he had been, but not mentioning the tide creeping in around Taffy, all alone there on the beach. But Grandpa told them not to give up hope. Perhaps, he said, perhaps when the tide comes in, the sand will loosen its hold, will get more watery, and he'll be able to haul himself out and come home.

'That cheered them a bit, but they were a sad lot going to bed that night, and your dad even said a prayer for Taffy. And in the morning, sure enough, there was Taffy, standing at the garden gate. He'd struggled out, and come home the fifteen miles by himself, in the dark.' She gave Biddy a hug, and pulled a dry beanie onto her head. 'And that's what Bella will do, too.'

Biddy couldn't bear to look at Bella as she climbed onto Blue and made herself a seat between the saddle-bags.

'Off you go, Bid. Go up along the side of the mob and tell Dad what's happened.' Lorna's voice had a catch in it. 'And stay up there with him. I'll bring the tail along.'

The quicker Biddy gets away from Bella the better, she thought. It was awful leaving her, half buried. She had stopped struggling now, and lay exhausted, her eyes dull, breathing in sighs. Despite the story of Taffy, Lorna knew there was a good chance Bella would drown.

Biddy booted Blue into a canter, and they splashed along the beach with the saddlebags thudding up and down. Bella whinnied desperately as they rode away, but when Biddy looked back her eyes were too blurred with tears to see anything more than a grey shape on the sand. Nearing her father she reined Blue in and wiped her eyes to look back again, but the sea-mist had swallowed the pony, and her cries grew fainter and fainter until they were lost in the crash of surf and keening bird calls.

13

Late home

Grandpa rocked Biddy gently with one arm and held a cup of hot chocolate to her lips with the other. The fire lit their faces, both stained with tears, as she told him what had happened.

That evening he had waited and waited. He knew she would be bursting with things to tell him. But as the night wore on it was clear some disaster must have befallen them. When finally the barking dogs told him the drovers had returned, he went out with the lantern and brought Biddy inside while her parents put away the horses and cattle.

Her face was grim. She wasn't sobbing, but the tears would not stop rolling down her face, so he wrapped her in a blanket and sat with her in front of the fire. Tigger landed lightly on her lap but she pushed him away.

'I've killed her. It's my fault. You told me to look out

for the quicksand and I didn't, and now Bella will drown.'

'Hey, girl,' Grandpa patted her hair. 'Don't be so hard on yourself. You're not the first to go into the quicksand, and you won't be the last. She still might come home. Did Mum tell you about Taffy?'

Biddy nodded. 'She'll be so frightened. I just wish I hadn't ridden out after those steers, so it didn't happen. Maybe if I'd been wider awake—'

Grandpa sighed. 'What's done is done. There's no turning back the clock. There's plenty of things I'd like to be able to do again, but that's not life. Come on, hop into bed and go to sleep. Your pony will more than likely be here when you wake up in the morning.'

Tigger jumped onto the bed and this time she let him stay, purring and pedalling into the blankets. Mum had brought her a hot water bottle when she came to say goodnight, and she held it against her stomach. The warmth seeped through her, but it didn't get to that cold patch in her heart. Losing Bella, losing Bella...

The wind was blowing from the east again. She could hear it groaning in the trees. It would be whipping the sand along the beach. She imagined the pony struggling as the cold waves beat against her, then pushed the picture from her mind.

A shadow fell across the floor as her father came to sit on the side of the bed. 'Goodnight, mate,' he kissed her hair gently. 'You did well. Really. You were a big help. And don't punish yourself. She'll be here in the morning. Wait on, I'll get something to cheer you up.'

He walked out into the passage and returned with Grandpa's bronze horse and set it on Biddy's chest of drawers. 'There. Look at him as you go off to sleep. That's what Bella will do. Goodnight, sweetheart.'

Biddy lay in bed, exhausted but not sleepy. Her body felt as if it was made of stone. She could hear snatches of conversation from the kitchen. Their voices were subdued, dull. Even the eight big bullocks, safely home and worth so much, weren't enough to change the mood.

'They've been lying to me,' Biddy said to Tigger. 'They don't really think she'll come home.'

Just then Grandpa turned on the light in his room and it shone across the passage and lit the bronze horse. He galloped up the beach in a blaze of light.

14

The next day

Something was dragging Biddy out of a long tunnel. She was so tired, dead tired, but something was insisting that she wake up. And then she remembered. Bella. She opened her eyes. The sun hadn't come up yet, but it was light enough to see.

She flew out of bed, dumping Tigger onto the floor, raced down the passage and out the back door, and there at the garden gate was . . . nothing. Maybe the pony was at the shed, or the yards. She ran, hobbling on the gravel track in her bare feet, not feeling the freezing wind, calling, calling, 'Bella! Bellaaaa!'

She looked behind the shed, the cypress trees, the chook house. Last year she had found Bella in the chook house, eating pellets, and Dad had joked that she might start laying eggs. She kept picturing the white pony, bedraggled and exhausted, but she was not there. Bella had not come home.

She walked back down the track to the house, not crying silent tears now but howling in despair. She slammed the back door and burst into her parents' bedroom. 'Bella hasn't come home! She's not here! I knew I should have stayed with her!' She kicked the wardrobe door. 'You knew she wouldn't be able to get out, didn't you? You told me bullshit so I'd come home, but you knew. I hate you both. All you care about are your cattle!'

She stayed in her room all morning, cursing and sobbing. She could hear her parents moving about the house and talking in the kitchen with Grandpa, but they left her alone.

At lunch time her father came in. Biddy looked up from the bed, her eyes red and swollen. 'I'm sorry, Dad. Sorry for saying that this morning.'

He stroked her hot head. 'Don't worry, mate. Listen, Bid, the tide will be out again now and your mother and I are going to drive back down the beach and have a look, just in case she managed to get free. Do you want to come? I'll understand if you don't.'

'Do you think there's still some hope?' Biddy's teary face showed a glimmer of excitement.

'No, I don't, to be straight with you. Not now. But I want to know for sure.' Her father always told the plain truth. 'I suppose we're looking for her body. That's why I said you might not want to come.'

'No, I'll come!' Biddy started to get dressed. Any chance was better than none.

The utility rolled smoothly along the beach. Normally Biddy stood up in the back, looking for shells, but she had no heart for it, even when her father stopped to collect a paper nautilus perched delicately on the sand. She wondered if she would feel like this for the rest of her life, as if nothing mattered.

'We should be there soon.' Dad patted her knee. 'That

big piece of driftwood was just after you caught up with me.' Biddy strained her eyes now, even though she was afraid of what she might see. In her mind there was a body half buried in the sand, or perhaps being buffeted around by the waves, but as they got closer there was nothing. No sign of a pony.

'It was right here, Dave,' Lorna's voice was sharp. 'See the sandbar. That's where she was. Stop and we'll have a look around.'

They stepped onto the sand and Biddy stared at the ocean. Was she out there, drowned and then swept away?

'Biddy! Lorna! Come up here!' Dad was standing high on the beach, where all the driftwood and seaweed washed up. They ran to him, labouring through the heavy sand.

'Look! Tracks!'

Biddy had to look at the sand for what seemed ages before the marks started to make any sense. She gasped aloud as she understood. There, coming out of the high tide mark, were Bella's hoofprints, but beside them were two other sets of tracks!

Footprints, small human footprints, and the paw marks of a dog.

'Well, I'll be blowed…' began Biddy's father.

'Mum,' whispered Biddy, 'my horse has been rescued by fairies.'

'Are you sure it was a footprint? A human footprint?' asked Grandpa, going over the story yet again as they ate dinner. 'There's no one out there. Just the ranger down at the station, and he hasn't got any kids. And old Dan. Are you sure it wasn't a…'

'I *saw* the tracks, Dad. We all saw them. We followed them up into the dunes until they petered out in that shaly country.' Biddy's father was poring over a map of the headland as he spoke. 'It's going to be hard looking for them. It's a mass of little gullies and paperbark swamps.'

'Who could be with her, though?' mused Lorna. 'Who could be that small and be out there?'

Biddy had hardly spoken since they found the tracks on the beach. All the way back in the ute she had sat between her parents, buzzing with the thought: Bella's alive, Bella's alive! Now she looked up from her plate, still beaming, and shocked her family. 'I know who's rescued Bella. I bet it's Joycie's baby.'

15

Joe alone

Joe never went back to the secret valley, to his home. He found himself at Middle Spring the morning after Joycie died and he stayed there a long time. He played with the dingo pup, fished in the lake, built a rough shelter, walked to the ranger's for supplies, and . . . waited for something to happen. He couldn't just walk up to the ranger, or in to town, and say, 'I'm Joe.' What if Joycie was right? Maybe it was dangerous.

He missed Jozz most at night, and he imagined how the valley would be without them. The little birds would be missing their scraps. The rabbits would have eaten all the silverbeet, without him there to fix the fence. He looked up at the moon. It would be so quiet. He and Joycie used to lie on the valley floor and watch the sugar gliders flying across the moon. They'd be flying tonight.

Without the pup, Joe would have died of loneliness. He called him Devil, after the Phantom's dog. The pup was a beautiful golden colour, paler at his throat, gangly and playful. He was learning to hunt already, patting fallen leaves with his paw to flush out lizards, then chasing them frantically through the long summer grass. He snuggled beside Joe at night, and sometimes woke him by gently brushing his whiskers on his face. He brought all his catches back to share—even though Joe didn't fancy mangled lizard. He expected Joe to share his food, too. If Joe didn't offer him some, even just a tiny piece, Devil would look at him, head tilted, as if to say, 'Well, have you forgotten your manners? What about me?' He didn't bark or whine, but his eyes and facial expressions always told Joe exactly what he thought.

One of his favourite games was to sneak up and steal some little thing, then race around like a lunatic while Joe tried to catch him. One night, as Joe dozed before the fire, Devil pulled his slippers off, then stood on the other side of the fire, grinning. He was dainty, clever, and very funny.

Later that summer, Joe moved to the estuary behind the Red Bluff. The fish and oysters were easy to get there and the nights were warm enough to sleep without shelter. Every evening a straggle of pelicans flew in from the ocean. They looked like ships floating down through the coloured sky. It made Joe laugh to see them land, their webbed feet splayed out, splashing, then settling gently onto the water.

When the weather got colder, and the days shorter, Joe and Devil travelled through the paperbark forests looking for a new home. No one ever came into this part of the headland. The scrub was as thick and tangled as

an old piece of fishing net. The tunnelled tracks that twisted through it were made by wombats and wallabies, and Joe had to bend double to pass along them. No bullock, horse or drover had ever been there.

He found a perfect spot, a gully deep in the marshes. Slightly higher than the surrounding wetland, like Joycie's valley, it caught all the northern sun. It was encircled by a sea of swordgrass so ancient that it had matted together, then grown up through itself. Joe had to clamber over the bottom layer, almost as tall as himself, and push through the thick secondary growth that towered above him. He hated going through it. The leaves cut his clothes and hands, and he knew it was full of snakes—tiger snakes probably—and they were the one thing on the headland that he was truly afraid of.

He built a wonderful thatched house there. Sheer granite boulders made two sides of it, and one of the rocks even had a trickle of water feeding into a natural basin at its base. Joycie would have thought that was pretty flash, having running water in the house. He jammed paperbark branches between the rocks, and wove swordgrass and smaller sticks through the branches. Then he dragged up mud from the swamp on a sheet of bark and pushed handfuls of it between the sticks and branches. When it dried, not a whisper of wind could get in. For the roof he laid more branches on top of the walls, then tied swordgrass and bark over the branches. The roof tilted slightly so the rain ran off and not many drops came through. He hung a bag in the doorway, weighing the bottom down with stones so that it wouldn't flap in the wind, and that was it. He had made his home.

There was just enough room inside for his bed, a table, and a small fireplace for the coming winter. He found a kerosene tin washed up on the beach and cut the front of it open to take small pieces of wood. It made the hut very warm, but the smoke nearly smothered him. The next time he walked to the store for supplies, he took an old bit of spouting from behind the ranger's hut and made a crooked chimney to carry the smoke away.

His bed was made of thick paperbark poles sitting on rocks with branches and grass on top of the poles. The big patchwork rabbit-skin rug Joycie sewed when he was little went doubled on top, and it was heaven to climb into at night. It still smelt of Joycie. When the house was finished he spent days slashing and burning a path so he didn't have to climb through the swordgrass all the time.

Devil was always beside Joe. Some nights they heard dingoes howling in the distance, and Devil would pace about the camp, but he never responded. He had become an excellent hunter, so they had meat to roast nearly every day. He didn't stalk his prey, but he was always on the lookout, and when he spotted something he was after it like a flash. Joe loved the sudden burst of speed he could put on, and if the rabbit or wallaby got away, Devil bounced on all fours to try and spot it. He looked so funny, flying up into the air, looking around everywhere. He carried his catch back to camp in his powerful jaws, presenting it to Joe like a gift.

But with every day Joe grew more and more curious about the other world. He read and re-read his battered books and comics. Without Joycie telling him all the time about the wickedness of men, the fear began to fade and curiosity took over. He wasn't scared any more, only wary. Joycie had talked of Mick and her dad with such love that he knew they'd welcome him.

The ranger didn't interest him. Joycie and he had shadowed the man and laughed at his ways so often that he seemed ridiculous. The people Joe was really interested in were the musterers, the drovers. In the autumn, when they brought the cattle to the headland again, he followed their every move. He listened to their conversations, patted their beautiful horses as they grazed at night, and imagined walking up to their camp-fire.

He made friends with the dogs, but his own dog, his dingo, vanished while the drovers were there. Even if he had felt brave enough to talk to them, he couldn't just leave Devil. He stole an oilskin coat. As he took it, he could hear Joycie telling him not to, but he had to have it. Winter was on its way, and his clothes were very thin. Besides, he heard the woman, Lorna, saying that it was·a spare one, that it was Biddy's. He knew that name. Joycie had told him the story of old Biddy, and shown him the cave she had sheltered in, but that was a long time ago. This must be a different Biddy.

16

Tracks!

Winter seemed to last forever. Every day was cold, and when the sun did shine it was too feeble to warm anything. The rain never let up. Joe lived in the oilskin coat. The nights seemed endless, and when dawn finally came, often he couldn't be bothered getting up. Everything was hard. Hunting was hard, cooking was hard, having a wash was hard. Going to the store, which was always such an adventure with Joycie, was now simply a necessity. Sometimes he lingered in the building and imagined not having to leave, just staying beside the warm stove.

He walked out to the surf beach on the first warm day. He thought he might have a swim to try and shake off the tiredness that lay on him. He and Joycie used to have such a good time out here. The purple flags were flowering. It must be his birthday. He didn't really care—Devil couldn't sing Happy Birthday, or make the food that Joycie made. He climbed wearily to the top of the dunes to look over the beach.

There were horse tracks on the sand! Four sets of tracks!

He looked down the beach, straining his eyes to pick up something through the sea-mist. Nothing. They must have passed by early this morning.

'Look, Devil! They're back!' He felt better straight away. 'Come on, let's follow them.' He began to run in the direction the horses had gone, skipping along the seaweed the way Joycie always made him, leaving no tracks. The dingo followed for a few paces, then turned back. He howled from the top of the dunes, and Joe stopped. 'I'm not staying just because you don't want to go,' he muttered half to himself. 'I'll see you at home.' He laughed as he hurried along the beach. Devil looked just like Joycie used to when he did something she didn't want him to.

Joe peered down through the banksia leaves at the cattle standing in the clearing.

'Saaalt! Saalt!' The voice came from just below him.

He nearly fell out of the tree. 'Come on! Saalt! Salt! Saaalt!' The noise was deafening. It was so loud after months of solitude. The cattle milled towards the call, and a horse and rider moved into his view. It was just a kid! A girl. A bit bigger than him, but not much. And the horse was a little one, too. Just his size. A beautiful little white horse with a long shining mane. Like the Phantom's horse, Hero.

The kid started to call again, and leaned down to tip small piles of salt onto the ground. Two golden plaits poked from under her beanie. They shone, even shinier than the horse's mane. Joe felt his own hair, long and matted, and not smelling that good either, he noticed. Joycie would be cross if she knew how dirty he'd got.

The cattle moved away from the tree to lick at the piles of salt, and Joe slid down the trunk and slipped into the scrub. He wriggled through the tea-tree and swordgrass until he was beside the packhorse.

'Hey, boy. How you doing?' Blue whinnied in recognition as Joe rested his head against the old horse's neck. He loved the feel of horses. They were so big and warm, so gentle. They smelt good. He felt under the flap on the pack-saddle. Oats, rope, pans, no, that wasn't what he was looking for. He felt in another pocket. Yes! His hand closed around a small, flat slab. Chocolate!

Joe stayed beside the old horse all afternoon, sucking on the chocolate bar, and watching the girl. He really liked the look of her and her little horse. It would be good to just step out of the bush and talk.

When Lorna drove her mob of steers into the clearing, his heart gave a little skip. He was pleased to see her, even if she didn't know he existed. He listened greedily to their conversation. So this was Biddy! And Lorna was her mum. He nearly burst trying to hold in his giggles when they started talking about Blue, and what was spooking the cattle.

He shadowed the cattle back to the holding yards, moving through the bush like a whisper. Top and Nugget came to him when the mob was moving quietly, wagging their tails and licking his hands. They were old friends. A whistle came and they raced away. Joe could hear them barking and the drovers shouting. 'Here! Push up! That's enough. Come here. Come here!' He ran ahead and climbed the stony ridge that overlooked the holding yards, so he was very close to the cattle and riders as they passed below.

'They look guilty. Don't you think, Biddy? Those two dogs have been up to no good.' Lorna reached over to Biddy and patted her back. 'They've been nicking off ever since we left the flat. I wonder...'

Biddy didn't answer. She looked tired, worn out. He knew that feeling. Sometimes when Joycie had taken him on a long day's hunting, he'd felt like that at the end of the day. Sometimes mums didn't realise how tired you got.

17

Time to leave

Joe leaned against Blue, soaking up his body heat. He gazed into the fire from the darkness. Biddy had been asleep for ages, snoring in her swag. Her parents sat together, their faces shining in the glow of the coals.

'I have to do it,' he thought. 'I have to go up and talk to them.' The thought of them going back up the beach without him made him feel sick. He didn't want to be left behind on the headland. He didn't want to be all alone. It might be scary back at the town, but it would be better than this. His hands plaited and fiddled with the old horse's mane as his mind raced. Joycie had taught him all sorts of fancy plaits.

He thought about Devil, about his house. If he went out to Lorna and Dave now, they mightn't let him go back to the gully. And he had to. All his things were there. The comics, the books, the blue-and-silver tin...

If he went there now, he could be back by tomorrow morning. And then he could come out of the bush and say . . . what? 'My name is Joe.' Maybe he'd just stand there.

He wriggled forward to where the pack-saddle lay on the ground and felt through the food bag. His hand closed around a packet of bacon. Mmm, he'd had this before, from the store. He'd go home, have a farewell feast with Devil, get his things, and be back by morning.

The moon disappeared behind the ridge just as he dropped into his gully. Lucky it lasted so long, he thought. The walk had been hard, but it would have been much worse in pitch dark. He was so tired. He moved like a zombie through the gloom. A shadow detached itself from the house and moved towards him.

'Devil. Good boy.' He crouched down and hugged the dingo to him. Devil sniffed and stepped back. A low growl rose from his throat. 'Hey, don't be like that. I haven't brought the dogs with me. It's just their smell.'

Joe pulled Devil's ears and rubbed the loose skin around his face. This was how their games usually started, but not tonight. Instead of pricking his ears and leaping away for Joe to chase him, the dingo walked back to the hut and lay down, settling his chin onto his paws with a sigh.

'You know, don't you? You know I'm going.' Joe sat beside him and ruffled the stiff yellow coat. 'You're such a smart dog. You always know what's happening. But I've got to go. You belong here, but I don't. I need to be with people.' A sob caught in Joe's throat. He pressed his face into Devil's neck and wiped his tears on the fur. 'Devil, I don't want to leave you.'

The dingo sat and watched him steadily while he made a small fire in the fireplace and fried the bacon. He didn't take his eyes off Joe as he moved in and out of the hut, gathering his things. Joe was so tired he couldn't think straight, and kept changing his mind about what he was taking and what he was leaving behind. He'd have to go as soon as they'd eaten the bacon. He groaned at the thought of the walk back to the holding yards. It was such a long way, and now the night was really black. The bacon smelt so good. Joe grabbed a piece out of the pan and ate it, burning his fingers and his mouth but too hungry to care.

'Ow! Mmmnn. Oh, that's delicious.' He tossed a rasher to Devil. 'Here, boy, here's a bit for you.' The dingo looked down his nose at the sizzling morsel as if to say, 'If that was the last food on earth, you traitor, I wouldn't eat it.'

Joe leaned against the side of his hut and pulled Devil to him. The fire warmed them as they nestled together. I'll just rest for a little while, he thought, just shut my eyes for a moment before I go.

When he had been asleep for a short time, Devil bent down and delicately picked up the bacon. He ate it with great care, licked every trace of fat from his muzzle, then settled his head and slept before the fire.

18

The rescue

Joe forced his eyes open. Where was he? Why was he outside his house, not in his snug bed? Dawn was breaking. Ugh, his body was stiff and sore. The first rays of sun were filtering into the gully and the scrub wrens were calling and flitting through the bush. *No!* He suddenly remembered. He should be back at the holding yards now, not here. He'd miss them! They'd go up the beach with the cattle and never even know he was here.

He grabbed the bag he'd packed last night. If he ran he might catch them. He'd heard Lorna say they had more mustering to do in the morning, before they left. 'Come with me, Devil. Come on!' he called to the dog. 'Keep me company some of the way.'

He started running along the gully floor, silently on the soft moss, and Devil loped behind him.

He ran for hours. Slipped, fell, got up, and ran again.

Through the swordgrass, across the marshes, along the tea-tree tunnels. If I just keep putting one foot in front of the other, he told himself, I can keep going. When he climbed across the boulders on the side of Windy Ridge he could see the sea sparkling out to the west. It was a beautiful day, clear and bright. They would have been up early.

He hurried along the ridge, leaping from rock to rock, and stopped at the last overhang to peer down towards the holding yards, looking for some movement, for a sign of life. He couldn't see the beach from here because it was blocked by the shoulder of the hill. Maybe they were out there already. Or they could still be mustering. He looked up at the sun; it was almost directly overhead. He'd have to go down to the camp to see.

He began to stumble off, then realised Devil wasn't following him. 'Oh, mate! Come here.' He dropped his bag and reached his arms out to the dingo, who jumped down to him. 'I'll never forget you, Devil.' He buried his face in the yellow fur and held him close for a moment. 'I can't stay. They'll be leaving.' Devil whined, but Joe pushed him away and crashed down the mountain side, his eyes blurred with tears; falling, rolling, scrambling.

He knew he'd missed them the minute he walked into the camp. Everything was gone. The fire had been doused. The stink of cattle was still there, though. Joe leaned against the yards and looked at the tracks that ran down to the river. He was so exhausted he felt as if he was somehow looking at himself standing there. He was so sad, so alone. He couldn't stay. He looked at the tracks again, wearily picked up his bag, and trudged out of the camp, following the cattle. He'd catch up with them.

The cattle tracks made the beach look dirty. Instead of smooth pale sand, it was dark and churned-up. It looked as if something terrible had happened, Joe thought. Well, it had. He'd missed his chance. Biddy and her parents had gone and he hadn't said hello. There was no sign of them in the distance. The tracks just ran into the sea-mist. He kept walking. He'd catch up, even if it wasn't until he got to their place. Something caught his eye and he bent to pick it up. It was Biddy's knitted hat. He pulled it on his head and smiled to himself. 'Ah, er, hello. I'm Joe. I found this on the beach, and I think it's yours.' He couldn't imagine where he would be standing when he said that.

He walked on in a daze, stopping occasionally to heave his bag onto the other shoulder. It was a beautiful day, and although the wind was cold, it was at his back, helping him up the beach. He watched a line of pelicans gliding and banking along the surf. He wondered if they were the pelicans from his summer camp. His eyes followed the birds as they flew away from him, out along the sandbar. What was that?

It looked like a lump of seaweed or driftwood, half buried, but as he strained his eyes to see, it seemed to move.

It *did* move!

The thought crossed his mind that it might be a stranded whale. Maybe it was a monster, or a bunyip. It looked pretty weird. It looked a bit like a horse.

He started to run along the sandbar, pausing now and then to try to see just what it was.

It *was* a horse. It was Bella!

The pony lifted her head feebly from the quicksand and whinnied to Joe. He sat his bag on the firm sand and waded through the slop to her.

'Oh, Bella! What's happened?' The pony looked half dead.

Joe sat down and cradled Bella's head in his lap, brushing the sand off her eyes and patting her. 'Why have they left you?' Maybe Biddy or someone was hurt. There must be a reason. Who'd leave a pony stuck like this? He looked behind him. The tide was almost right out now, but soon it would be turning. Bella would drown if he couldn't get her out. He scooped up a handful of quicksand. Instantly more sand oozed into the space he made.

'Oh, Bella, I don't know if I can do this.' He leaned into her neck. Why was everything so hard? What would Joycie do?

He thought, then remembered the time he'd asked her about the shell necklace, the necklace from Seal Island. How, he had asked, how could anyone have threaded all those shells, hundreds of shells? Little bit at a time, Joycie had smiled, little bit at a time. He patted Bella, then whispered into her ear. 'I'm going to get you out, pony, if I have to dig all day.'

Joe didn't know how long he'd been digging. He lay beside Bella and scooped handfuls of quicksand, one at a time, and flung them onto the hard sand. He used his right arm until it ached, and then he used his left arm. When it started hurting he swapped back to his right arm. He didn't seem to be making any headway. The sand oozed back into every hole he dug. But, he thought, it had to be doing some good. He leaned against Bella's neck and rested for a moment in the afternoon sun. The tide had started to come in. The first flat sheets of water were creeping over the sandbar, but Joe didn't notice. He slept by Bella's side.

A familiar feeling woke him—the touch of whiskers on his face. Devil! Joe opened his eyes, and it *was* Devil, grinning at him and wagging his tail. His foxy look, Joe called it. He looked like this when he thought he was being very clever.

'Devil! You followed me! I'm so glad to see you!' Joe looked behind him and was shocked to see water over the sandbar. 'Come on, mate, help me dig.' He sank on his knees into the bog, and dug like a dog, throwing the sand out behind him. 'Come on, Devil, like this.'

Devil watched for a moment, head on one side, puzzled.

'Come *on*, you dumb dog! Dig!'

A flicker crossed Devil's eyes. He knew he'd been

insulted. He turned and started to dig beside Joe.

The first big wave came without warning, flooding into the quicksand. Joe was so absorbed in his task that he didn't hear it coming. The icy water shocked him. Devil leapt back, and Bella snorted with fright. When the wave receded Joe looked at the bog in despair. 'We haven't made any difference, Devil. All that digging, and she's stuck the same as when I found her.' He floundered back to Bella's head and hugged it, crying with frustration. 'I'm sorry, Bella. I'm sorry.'

As the sea rushed around them he held Bella's head up, out of the water. He couldn't believe this was happening, that she was going to drown. Devil backed towards the shore, whining, wanting him to come out. 'I can't leave her!' Joe yelled at him, 'I can't leave her to drow—'

A wave swept right over them. Water filled his eyes and mouth. He coughed, choking, and twisted his fingers through Bella's mane to pull her head as high as he could. Only her eyes and nostrils were out of the water now. Joe heaved on her mane.

What was that?

She moved! He pulled again, and this time felt a

definite shift. The water must be loosening the quick-sand! It was releasing her.

'Come on, Bella, fight! Come on, struggle!'

He kept dragging on the silver mane. The waves were getting bigger. Each one knocked him down, but Bella was rising, was floating out of the quicksand. He felt her begin to kick feebly. Her cramped and frozen legs found strength and suddenly she was free!

Joe didn't let go of her mane. He wasn't going to lose her now. He guided her as the waves chased them to the shore, where Devil ran up and down, yipping frantically. Bella's legs wobbled as she walked up the beach. 'Keep going, Bella. Keep walking.' Joe steered her towards a gap in the dunes. He had to get her off the beach and out of the wind. He hardly noticed Devil. He had to keep Bella moving. The ocean roared behind them. We beat you, he thought. We got away.

Bella just made it. Every step in the loose sand was a huge effort. Her breathing was harsh and uneven. Finally they were behind the dunes, out of the freezing wind, and Joe collapsed to the ground. He felt as if he would disintegrate like the sand; just fall into thousands of tiny pieces.

The sky was darkening. Bella stood where he'd let her stop, her head down, and her sides heaving. Her eyes were very dull. I'll have to fetch her a drink, Joe thought. I'll get my billy and bring her some water from the creek.

'Oh, no!' He remembered he'd left his bag on the sand where Bella was bogged. The thought flattened him. It was too much. All his things, all his life, everything he'd gone back for, had missed Biddy and her parents for, had run so far for; it was all gone. He put his head in his hands and wept.

He felt Devil's whiskers on his arm, and looked up. He was doing that look again, that foxy look he did when he thought he'd been very clever. Joe broke into a huge smile and kissed the dingo right on his big black nose. He *was* clever, very clever. He was holding Joe's bag in his jaws.

19

Who?

'What do you mean, Joycie's baby?' Lorna asked sharply. 'We've never told you about Joycie. Have you been—'

'Irene told me,' Biddy blurted quickly. 'The day you said I could go on the muster. We were talking at school, and she told me about Joycie and Joe. She reckons they never drowned, that they went to live on the headland—'

'But that was *nine years* ago,' Biddy's father cut in. 'They couldn't have lived out there for all that time.'

'Yes they could,' replied Biddy. 'They could of eaten grubs and berries and stuff, like Biddy the convict did.'

Lorna snorted. 'They'd be pretty skinny if they'd been eating berries and grubs for nine years. And it's could *have*, not could *of*.'

Biddy pushed her chair aside and walked across to the stove. She hated it when Lorna treated her like a little kid. She stood with her back to the room, pretending to warm her hands on the heat from the Aga, but really hiding her face from the adults. She could see her reflection in the shiny lids, burning red. It was suddenly very important that her family listened, listened seriously. She took some deep breaths, then, when she could trust her voice not to break, she started to speak, still keeping her back to the room.

'You just don't want to believe that it could be true, but think about all the things that have happened ... I reckon they have been watching us while we were down at the headland. I reckon they stole the bacon the night before last.'

She turned from the stove as her father began to speak. 'No, it wasn't Top.' She looked down at Tigger, who was doing figure-eights around her legs. 'Top was in my swag. I was using him as a hottie. Anyway, what about the plaits? Who plaited the horses? And plaited them the same way that Irene plaits? Irene's aunty, that's who.'

Dave scratched his head. 'Look, mate, I know what you're saying makes sense, but I just can't believe a girl and a little baby could survive in the bush for nearly nine years. It doesn't seem possible.'

'They wouldn't be a girl and a baby any more, Dad,' Biddy cut in. 'Joycie would be twenty-six, and Joe would be nine. You have to say it's *possible*, at least. Don't you reckon, Pa?'

Grandpa ran his gnarled hands slowly over his face and sighed. 'Hmmnn.'

'What? What do you mean, "hmmnn"?' asked Biddy. 'Tell us, Grandpa.'

'Well, I don't know how to say this without looking like a complete fool, but I'll say it anyway. I haven't been out to the headland for, let's see, three years, but there were times in those last trips when I could swear someone was watching me. You know, when the hairs stand up on the back of your neck. Perhaps it was Joycie. There. You can send me off to the nut-house, if you like, but I'll stand by what I've said.'

Biddy put her arms around his bony shoulders and glared at her parents. 'See. I'm not just imagining it. Grandpa thinks Joycie and Joe have rescued Bella too.'

'But if that's true,' said Lorna, 'how come there was only one set of footprints beside Bella's tracks? Little ones, too. Why was Joe by himself? Where was Joycie?'

'I know what we should do!' shouted Biddy suddenly.

'We should ring Irene and her mum and dad and tell them.'

'No, Biddy!' Her mother's voice was harsh. 'They mustn't know anything about it.'

'Why not? They'll be so excited—'

'That's just why we can't tell them. Because they'll be so excited. Imagine how terrible it would be for them if they got their hopes up and it turned out to be nothing.' Lorna's eyes filled with tears. 'They've already gone through the pain of losing Joycie and Joe, all those years ago. We couldn't make them do it again.'

Grandpa patted Biddy's back. 'Your mother's right. Let's keep it quiet. We'll go down to the headland tomorrow and have a bit of a poke around and see what we can find. Here, bring that map over and I'll show you where I think you should look.'

When Joe woke up he didn't know where he was. He hardly knew *who* he was. His sleep had been filled with dreams, dreams of horses, dogs, cattle, Joycie, and him running, always running, and never getting there. He rubbed his eyes and sat up. It was cold in his house. He remembered then that he'd draped his rabbit-skin rug over Bella last night. Bella! A terrible fear struck him—that she might have died while he was asleep. Her breathing sounded awful by the time they'd got back last night.

He pushed aside the bag in the doorway, almost afraid to look. She wasn't there. He stepped outside and put his hand up to shield his eyes from the sun. It was late. He must have slept nearly all day.

As his eyes adjusted, Joe heard a twig snap and looked to the edge of the clearing. His worries vanished. There was Bella, by the swordgrass, grazing peacefully. Devil sat beside her. He looked up as Joe walked towards them, as if to say, 'I like her and she likes me, too.' Joe felt as light as air.

The rabbit-skin rug had hardly shifted on Bella. Joe felt underneath it, and she was warm and dry. She stopped grazing for a moment to nuzzle at his pockets. She had kept doing that to him last night when they were coming through the tea-tree. It had taken ages. The branches were so low that Joe had to push or break nearly every one to make the tunnel big enough for Bella. She had stood behind him patiently, just nudging him with her nose from time to time. It had been so good to get to the path in the swordgrass, and then to get home. His house had looked welcoming in the moonlight, but Joe had been too tired to make a fire. He'd just tied the rug on Bella and slept.

Bella nudged him again, this time in the belly. His insides felt tender, and he realised how hungry he was. He could eat a horse, as Joycie used to say. He smiled. 'Come on, you two. I'll make some damper for tea.'

He walked along the valley, picking up sticks for his fire as he went. The pony and the dingo followed him, and the three of them shone in the golden evening light.

20

Bolting horses

Biddy sat on Blue, one foot crossed over the front of her saddle. Her father told her not to do it. 'If that horse gets a fright, you'll go over backwards. You will, you'll go bum over breakfast.'

Biddy laughed. She loved it when she and Dad were together. 'Mum does it all the time,' she pointed out, 'and you don't tell her not to do it.'

'It would take a braver man than me to tell your mother what to do. Anyway, she can ride,' he teased. 'She's not just a little beginner like you.'

He laughed as he handed her Gordon's reins. 'You wait here with the horses. Don't go anywhere, understand. I'll be a while. I want to follow this stony ridge, and it's too steep for the horses. I might be able to spot something from the top.'

He reached into the pocket of his oilskin coat and

pulled out a handful of mints. 'Here, these should keep you busy. I'll see you soon. Now, what do you have to do?'

Biddy screwed up her face, and said slowly, as if she was reciting tables, 'Wait . . . here . . . don't . . . go . . . anywhere.'

'Good girl.'

Dave patted Gordon on the rump, turned, and vanished into the bush.

Biddy could hear her father crashing through the timber for a while, and soon it was quiet. And then, from the silence, grew tiny bush sounds: birds, the breeze in the scrub, the horses' breathing, a fly bumbling past. It was amazing how much noise there was in silence. She

wondered if Mum and Grandpa had arrived yet in the ute. She and Dad had ridden down this morning and led Mum's horse, Dusky. It felt just as scary, riding over the cliff path the second time.

Mum would drive down, when the tide had gone out far enough. Grandpa refused to be left behind, so they decided he could come in the ute. Biddy and her father had tethered Dusky to a bush, close to where Bella had disappeared. Lorna was going to leave Grandpa in the ute, on the beach, with a thermos and sandwiches, and then ride along the back of the dunes, searching for tracks. Grandpa had been given even stricter instructions than Biddy about staying put.

Biddy put her foot back over the saddle. It looked good when Lorna did it—she looked really relaxed—but it didn't feel that good for Biddy. She twisted in the saddle and tried her other foot. That was worse. She spun around so that she was sitting backwards on Blue. Hey! She was doing around-the-world. They used to do this at Pony Club, when she was little. She and Irene were in red group together. Biddy thought about Irene, and going around to her place. 'Guess what, Rene?' she'd say. 'You know your cousin, Joe . . . '

Biddy snapped out of her daydream as Gordon suddenly pulled backwards. 'Whoa, boy, whoa!' she called to him, hanging onto the back of her saddle. She had dropped Gordon's reins and they were tangled around a low branch. Every time Gordon moved, the branch moved too, and the horse was panicking. 'Stand still, you stupid horse!'

Biddy leaned across to free him, but as she did, a rosella flew out of the bush, right beside Gordon's face, and it was too much for him. He went crazy, pulling back in one direction and then the other, pounding his hooves into the earth, snorting and rolling his eyes. Suddenly, with a crack, the branch broke, and this terrified him even more. Every time he moved back it followed him. Gordon's eyes were bulging out of his head. He looked at the branch as though it were a monster, then whirled around and galloped off with it bouncing beside him. Blue spun as well, dumping Biddy from her backwards position, and chased after Gordon, whinnying like a lunatic.

Biddy landed flat on her back, and the fall knocked the wind out of her. She lay on the ground, trying to breathe, listening to the horses bolting back to the beach. As her eyes filled with tears the leaves waving above her blurred into the sky. Bloody, bloody horses, she thought. If Gordon was supposed to be such a good horse, why did he act like a half-wit when she was looking after him? And Blue, she sniffed and wiped her nose on the back of her hand; who did he think he was, nicking off like that?

Her dad would skin her alive. It was ages back to the beach. And when the rotten horses did get there, Lorna and Grandpa would think there had been an accident, and worry themselves sick. Biddy was so angry she felt like exploding. She'd mucked up everything again. She'd made things harder instead of easier. She stood with her hands on her hips, looking bitterly along the track where the horses had bolted. 'I hate you both!' she screamed, but her voice sounded shrill in the silence.

21

Joe and Bella

Joe knew that he should be leaving, should be taking Bella up the beach to where Biddy and her parents lived, but it was perfect in his valley so he decided to stay one more day. Anyway, it would be good for Bella to have another day to rest. The morning was sunny and still and he'd woken up with a full belly, full of damper from last night. The walk to the farm didn't seem nearly as bad now he had Bella to share it with.

He ran his hand over Devil's ears. 'I really am going tomorrow, boy. This is our last day together.'

Devil didn't seem too worried, and Joe couldn't blame him. Their goodbyes were going on forever.

Bella nibbled the grass beside the log Joe was sitting on; tearing, chomping and snorting now and again, as though an insect had flown up her nose. She nudged him and he slipped forward off the log, laughing. 'You look so much like the Phantom's horse, I think I'll change your name. From now on you're Hero. Hero! Come here, Hero!'

The pony walked around the log to where he lay and began to graze near him. Her warm horsy breath tickled his neck. He giggled, not just from the tickling, but because he could trust her to stand so close yet so carefully over him.

He noticed that her belly and legs were caked with dried mud. Her mane was tangled and knotty, too.

'I reckon you need a clean-up, horse,' he said. He felt his own hair. 'I reckon we both do.'

Joe led Bella down to the stream, then walked her into the water. When they got to the deepest part and the water reached his chest, the cold made him gasp, but Bella didn't mind. 'Good girl, Bell—er, Hero. Now it's rub-a-dub-dub time.' He set to work with the soap, foaming up her mane and her tail, all along her back, down her legs and under her belly. He soaped himself all over, too, then climbed onto Bella and washed her mane again. He swam underneath her, then climbed on and slid down again, like a seal off a rock.

Devil sat on the bank, his head tilted, puzzled, but enjoying the show.

'Watch this!' Joe yelled. 'Watch us be a whale!' He lay on Bella and squirted a mouthful of water up to the sky, then flopped into the stream. Bella pawed the water, sending up huge splashes that made Devil scurry out of range.

When they were both clean and rinsed, a shivering Joe led the pony out of the stream. She shook the water from her coat in a spray that made a rainbow for one brief second, then folded her legs and lay down on the grass. First she rubbed all one side, from her neck to her hindquarters, then, grunting and groaning, she rocked and rolled over to her other side. Finally she clambered to her feet, had another huge shake, and looked at Joe as if to say, 'Mmmm, that feels good.'

As the sun dried her coat, Joe combed her mane and tail with his old tortoise-shell comb, carefully working out the tangles and knots until the hair flowed free. It made him think of Joycie's beautiful hair. He tried to comb his own, but it was just too matted, so he used Joycie's good scissors to cut it off. He kept snipping and snipping until there was nothing for the scissors to cut.

He ran his hands over his scalp, feeling the bristles. His head felt light and exposed, but there was also a wonderful feeling of freedom, of shaking off a burden and starting again.

22

A single white hair

Biddy sat and waited for her father. She dreaded telling him what a mess she'd made. She wished she could fix things up. Maybe she could. Maybe the horses hadn't gone all the way to the beach. Blue was such a pig, Biddy was sure he'd stop to graze if he came across some good grass.

She started imagining what would happen... She'd walk back to that little flat they passed on the way in, and Blue and Gordon would be there. Gordon's bridle wouldn't be broken, and she'd catch them easily, and ride Blue back, and lead Gordon, and she'd be sitting there as though nothing had happened when Dad got back. She wouldn't even have to tell him what had gone wrong. Maybe she'd tell him when she was really old.

Her father's voice echoed in her head. *Wait here. Don't go anywhere.* Biddy ignored it. She'd easily get to the flat and back before he returned. She set off at a brisk walk, and immediately felt better to be moving. The further she walked, the fainter her father's voice became.

She got to the flat quicker than she expected, but there were no horses, just deep hoofprints where they had galloped through. It looked as though they'd been really flying, the mongrels. 'I'll never forgive you for this, Blue, never,' Biddy growled to herself. 'I'll never give you carrots again.'

She trudged despondently back along the track to wait for her father. Wrens were darting through the bush, but she didn't notice. Her eyes were down, staring at the hoofprints those stinking horses had left.

Hang on, why was that set of prints going *across* the track? Biddy stepped back, to get a better look, then realised that a horse had plunged off the side. The tea-tree made a thick screen on both sides of the track, and when Biddy looked closer she could see that the slope fell away steeply on one side. She could see, too, where a horse had skidded down through the bushes. She inspected the branches closely and, yes, there was a single white hair.

Bella! It had to be Bella! She jumped through the gap

and slid down the sandy slope on her oilskin, like someone on a toboggan, whooping all the way. At the bottom
she was sure. The soil was damp here, and she could see
the tracks clearly: hoofprints, pawprints and footprints.
She was going to find Bella!

Her father's instructions crossed her mind again,
nagging at her conscience, but she pushed them aside. It
wouldn't matter so much about losing the other horses if
she found Bella. And Joe... She felt a bit nervous about
Joe. What if he didn't want her to find him? What if he
was nasty? What if he smelt awful? Would Joycie be
mad? She shrugged her shoulders and kept following the
tracks. She'd messed up everything so far—now she had
to keep going and turn it into something good.

The tracks led into a forest of tangled tea-tree, along a
tunnel that twisted like a worm. Biddy had to bend over
to fit through, and her back was soon killing her. Now
she knew how Grandpa felt, with his aches and pains. A
lot of branches had been broken or pushed aside. Joe
must have done that to get Bella through. Biddy could
imagine her, biffing Joe with her nose as he worked.

She knew she'd have to turn back soon. She stopped
to listen every now and then, in case her father was

calling, but the wind had come up and was roaring through the tea-tree, drowning out everything else. I'll walk for a hundred more steps, she thought, and then I'll turn back. She took big ones, so she could go as far as possible within the bargain, and at eighty-nine she stepped out of the tunnel into the afternoon light.

The tracks crossed a shallow creek, fringed with ferns and reeds, then disappeared into a mass of swordgrass. Biddy crossed the creek, ninety-three, ninety-four— Suddenly she could see a path through the swordgrass. It was a real path. A path somebody had made. She forgot her bargain and hurried along.

The swordgrass waving high above blocked out the sun. All she could hear was the rustle of dry leaves under her feet. Biddy began to call as she walked along, softly at first, then working up to a shout: 'Bella ... Bellaa ... Bellaaa.'

When she stopped to get her breath, she heard a whinny. It couldn't be. She called again. Yes! It was Bella answering her. She could hear hoofbeats, too. Bella was galloping towards her. And there was another noise as well: someone up ahead was calling a name over and over. Biddy couldn't work out what it was. Suddenly, in a flurry of hooves and flying mane, Bella flew around the corner and propped in front of her.

23

Biddy and Joe

Biddy never knew you could cry so much with happiness. She pressed her face against Bella's velvety nose, rubbed her ears, and hugged her and hugged her. The voice kept calling from where Bella had come. It sounded so strange that Biddy suddenly felt scared, afraid to meet Joycie and Joe. I'll go back, she thought. I'll take Bella back to Dad and then we can all come here together. 'Come on, Bella, let's go.'

She started to walk back along the path, her arm over Bella's neck, then turned in surprise as the pony stopped. 'Come on, girl.' Bella *always* followed her. 'Good girl, Bella, let's go.' Bella didn't budge. Biddy took a handful of mane. 'Come *on*, Bell, come on, girl,' she pleaded, pulling her mane. But the pony would not move.

Biddy's happy tears turned to tears of frustration. The weird voice was still calling, over and over, and it was coming closer all the time. Biddy felt terrified. 'Come *on*, Bella! This is serious!' She walked behind the pony and smacked her on the rump, trying to drive her away from that creepy voice.

'Don't! Don't do that!' Suddenly Joe was there, facing her over Bella's rump. Biddy knew her mouth was open, that she was gawking, but she couldn't help it. He was so *clean*. She'd expected him to look like a wild animal, hairy and dirty, but he was polished like an apple. His hair was really short. It was like the haircut she had given Tigger when she was little: short but uneven. He looked terrified, as though he'd run any minute, and he was hanging on to Bella like a limpet.

She smiled at him but his face didn't change. He looked past her anxiously. 'It's all right,' Biddy said softly, 'there's only me. I'm by myself.' She smiled at him again and this time he smiled back. He had a beautiful smile. 'Joe?' He nodded, and Biddy reached across Bella's back, offering him her hand. 'I'm Biddy.' Joe looked at her hand. 'You're supposed to shake it. Shake hands. It's what people do when they say hello.'

He smiled again and grabbed her hand. Biddy winced. Joe was smaller than her, but his hand felt as calloused and strong as her father's. He shook her hand up and down.

'That's okay. You can stop now,' Biddy told him. 'You only do it for a little while.' She took her bruised hand back and glanced over her shoulder. She half expected Joycie to come roaring along the track. Biddy bet she'd be like one of those big scary mothers at school who yelled at you if you picked on their kids. She must be pretty crazy to have lived out here all this time. She turned back to Joe. 'Hey! That's my—' She was going to say, 'that's my oilskin coat,' but she bit her lip. It was the one Lorna had lost last autumn, but she didn't want to scare Joe away by accusing him of stealing. He was rubbing Bella gently around her ears, and the pony looked as if she was in heaven.

Biddy pushed aside a little twinge of jealousy. 'Thanks for saving her.'

Joe smiled again. He looks so like Irene, Biddy thought. Same smile, same skinny brown arms, except Joe's were covered with scars and scabs. I bet when his hair grows it's black and crinkly like Irene's.

'She's good. She's tough. Devil likes her, too.' His voice was soft and mumbled, and Biddy thought he was talking about his mother.

'Where is she?' Her voice sounded like a foghorn compared to his. 'Why were you on your own when you rescued Bella? Where's Joycie?'

Joe looked at his fingers sliding through Bella's woolly coat. He was silent for a little while, then he murmured something that Biddy didn't catch.

'What?' she asked, reaching to stroke Bella's neck. 'What did you say?'

Joe looked up and into her eyes. 'She died.'

Biddy didn't know what to say. She stared at the ground for what seemed ages and when she looked up Joe was doing the same thing. He was sniffing. Biddy thought he wouldn't want her to think he was crying, so she started talking. 'I'm sorry. Are you all right? What happened to her? Umm, er, what did she die of? You don't have to tell me if you don't want to. You must have been lonely...' Her voice trailed off.

'I think it was about a year ago.' Joe was still looking at the ground, but he'd stopped sniffing. 'She just got sick and died. You talk a lot.'

Biddy smiled and looked up at the sky. It was tinged with pink. She suddenly thought of her parents. Dad had said that they'd have to leave at sunset to get the ute around the beach. She looked at Joe. 'How long does it take to get to the beach from here?'

'A while.'

'No, I mean in hours. How many hours would it take?'

Joe shrugged. 'Don't know. Don't know hours. Joycie taught me, but we never had a clock.'

Biddy felt stupid. 'Well, could we get to the beach before dark?'

Joe shook his head. 'No. Too far.'

Biddy rested her arms over Bella's back. Her parents would kill her. She'd done everything wrong. She'd got Bella bogged, then let the horses go and now she'd disappeared. She hoped the worry wouldn't make Grandpa sick. Surely they'd go home, and come back tomorrow morning?

She felt a touch on her back, light as a feather. It was Joe's hand. 'You all right . . . Bid . . . Biddy?' he asked.

Now it was Biddy's turn to sniff. 'Yeah. Thanks, Joe. Just worried about my mum and dad and Grandpa.'

Joe gave her one of his lovely smiles. 'Come on. Come back to my place. We'll walk out in the morning. You can meet Devil.'

He turned and Bella followed him. So much for my

loyal horse, thought Biddy. She had to jog to keep up with Joe. He had a strange gliding walk, almost silent, as though he hardly touched the ground.

'Who's Devil?'

'My dog. My dingo.' Joe stopped, and Biddy took the opportunity to vault onto Bella's back. She'd felt like a little kid, tagging behind him. On Bella, she felt like a princess. They walked on.

'Devil's shy. He might not like you.' Biddy felt miffed again. Of course his dog would like her. Just then the path opened on to the valley. Joe stopped again and whistled twice; low whistles that Biddy could barely hear. Nothing stirred.

24

Joe's house

Biddy thought Joe's home was the best house she'd ever seen. She'd made cubbies, but they were always flimsy things that fell down; just play houses. This was proper. She tried out the bed, sat on the chair, examined the stove. 'I feel like Goldilocks,' she laughed, then stopped suddenly. 'Sorry. You probably don't know about Goldilocks.'

'Yes I do.' Joe pulled a tin of books from under his bed. 'Look, here's the story. It was one of my best ones when I was little.' The pages were soft and faded, but there wasn't a rip or a crease.

Underneath the books was a pile of comics. They were so old they felt like cloth. 'Hey! *The Phantom!* I love these comics. Irene always gets them.' Biddy flipped through the first one and idly read a page.

'So that's what you were calling Bella this afternoon:

Hero. You were calling her Hero.' She pointed at a drawing of the Phantom's white horse. 'D'you reckon you're
the ghost-who-walks?'

Joe blushed. 'She didn't mind. But you call her what
you like. Why Bella, anyway?'

'It means beautiful.'

Joe put the comics and books away. 'That suits her.
That's much better than Hero.'

Biddy walked outside and almost stepped on a dead
rabbit lying beside Joe's campfire. 'Why would a rabbit
die there?' she asked.

Joe started to giggle.

'What's so funny? What? Tell me.'

'It didn't die there.' He was nearly bursting with
laughter. 'Devil left it. It's our dinner.'

Biddy's father crested the last rise before the beach. He
had run all the way back, but the heavy sand of the
dunes slowed him to a walk. He was angry with Biddy
for not being where he'd left her, but at the same time he
felt sick with worry. What could have made the horses
bolt like that? As he ran, he faltered at every bend, half
expecting to find Biddy lying crumpled around the turn,

but it hadn't happened. She must have stuck on. He looked down to the beach where Lorna was holding the three horses beside the ute. Gordon and Blue were streaked with dried sweat. They must have been going like the wind.

'Is she all right?' he called. Lorna cupped her hand to her ear. Dave raced down the dune in giant sliding steps and ran towards her. 'Is she all right?' he asked again, trying to see past the horses, into the ute. Grandpa was sitting in the passenger seat with his arm hooked over the door. Dave could almost see Biddy sitting there beside him.

Lorna stepped in front of him. 'What do you mean?' She grabbed his arm. 'Biddy's not here. I thought she was with you. The horses came back alone.'

Dave couldn't take it in. He pushed past her and peered through the open window. There was nothing on the seat but the thermos.

'So you've never been anywhere but the headland?' Biddy sucked her fingers clean and put the last rabbit bone on the pile beside her. She was saving them for Devil.

Joe hugged his knees. 'No. This is it. Mum always said

there were too many bad people. My dad got killed in the town.'

Biddy had to lean forward to hear his voice above the crackle of the fire. 'I know. I know that story from Irene.' She had told Joe that his cousin was her best friend. 'But you musn't think that would happen again. Most people are kind, like us.'

Bella was cadging damper from Joe, reaching over to pick the pieces from his lap. Joe leaned against her, his eyes closed. He looked so tired, thought Biddy, so small and tired. 'Are you scared?' she asked. 'I mean about the town. You are going to come back with me, aren't you?'

Joe nodded and looked into the fire. 'I've been following you all the time. I was going to talk to you the night before last, but I wanted to get my things. I thought your mum and dad mightn't let me come back. Then I missed you yesterday— Hey! I just remembered something.' He darted into his house. Biddy couldn't get used to the way he moved so fast and silently. 'Look!' He came out wearing her beanie. 'I found this on the beach.'

'Hey! My hat! Thanks, Joe.' She went to grab it, but he skipped out of her reach.

'Finders keepers. That's what Jozz used to say.'

Biddy chased him around the fire, first one way and then the other. She had no hope of catching him; he was as fast and slippery as an eel. She plopped onto her log, panting and laughing. 'I give in. You can keep it.'

'No, I was only playing,' Joe wrapped the hat around a stick and tossed it across the fire to Biddy, but before she could catch it, a yellow shape—an animal—flashed past and the hat was gone. Biddy screamed. Joe hurried around the fire to her. 'It's okay. That was Devil. He couldn't help himself. His favourite game is keepings-off.'

Biddy stirred. She and Joe were curled together under the rabbit-skin rug, but something was waking her. Something was tickling her face. She opened her eyes and froze. A pair of amber eyes stared at her from the edge of the bed. 'Hello, Devil,' Biddy whispered. The dingo dropped the hat onto the bed, then settled beside the door. He gave Biddy a friendly look, and rested his head on his paws. 'Goodnight, Devil. Nice to meet you,' she said softly. Then she, too, drifted back to sleep.

25

Irene

Irene shut the chook-house door, then peered into the dark to make sure the catch was secure. She heard a car pull up at the front of the house and hurried around to see who was there. It was the Frasers. Good, Biddy could tell her about the muster.

'Hi, Mr Fraser, Mrs Fraser, Old Mr Fraser.' She and Biddy always called each other's grandfathers Old Mr Fraser and Old Mr Rivers, so they didn't mix them up with their fathers.

'Evening, Irene.' Biddy's father didn't smile. Usually he made a big fuss of Irene and called her McGerk. Biddy was Erk and she was McGerk. 'Is your father home?'

'Yes.' Irene led them up the front steps. 'Where's Biddy? Why isn't she with you?' Nobody answered.

The door opened, spilling inside light onto the verandah, then all the adults were talking at once:

quicksand, Bella, bogged, Biddy, lost, Joycie, Joe, tracks...

Irene tugged her mother's sleeve. 'Are they alive, Mum? Has Biddy found them?'

'Be quiet. Let me listen.' Her mum shoved her little brother into her arms. 'Take Tom and read him a story.'

There was no way Irene was leaving the room. She sat Tom on the sink and fed him bits of banana—anything to keep him quiet while she listened.

'Do you think she's met up with them? With Joycie and Joe?' Irene heard her father ask.

Dave took off his hat and ran his hand over his head. 'I don't know. I think I'd have found her if she'd been hurt. And I made it clear she was to stay put. Really drummed it into the little beggar.'

'She must be with them,' Lorna's voice cut in, softer than normal. 'That's the only reason she'd disobey you. I think she's gone with Bella and Joycie and Joe.' She turned to Irene's father. 'This is a terrible question, Mick, but do you think Joycie would harm her? Would she chase her away?'

'No. You've got nothing to worry about there.' Irene's father started to roll a map out on the table. 'I don't care

how loopy she might have got, she wouldn't hurt any-
body. She's just too gentle.'

Irene cleared the plates off the table to make a space
for the map. 'Good girl.' Her dad passed her the bowls.
Whew, thought Irene, I'm not invisible any more. She
hated the way parents ignored you when something
serious was going on. She bumped Tom onto her hip and
stood behind her grandfather. He was very pale.

'It's almost nine years.' His voice wavered. 'Nine years.
It'd be a bloody miracle. It'd be like getting her back from
the grave.'

Biddy's grandfather pulled out his pipe and started to
light it. 'Don't go putting the cart before the horse, my old
mate. It might not be them. We've only seen one set of
tracks, remember. Let's have a look at this map.'

The two old men reached into their top pockets and
put their glasses on exactly the same way. Irene smiled,
and her father caught it. 'That's right. Like an old married couple, they're that alike.' He spun the map to face
them.

'Now. We've got three horses down there, low tide at
four a.m., and what should be a fairly clear set of prints.
And,' he tapped his fingers on the table, then pointed to

Mick and Pops, 'we've got two of the best trackers south of the divide. Let's be down there, so we can start looking at first light.'

'Do you think we should tell anyone?' asked Irene's mother. 'Should we tell the police?'

'And what do you think the police are going to do?' Pops had been feuding with the local policeman for years. 'You know, Jean, who they'd get to lead the search, don't you?'

'Yeah. You and Mick. I know. Righto then, let's keep this to ourselves.' She pushed back her chair. 'Give Tom to me, Irene. You'd better get to bed.'

Irene stomped across the room and dumped the little boy on her mother's lap. She could feel tears getting ready to burst out of her eyes. It was so unfair. Why was she always left out? 'I don't see why I can't go. Biddy's my best friend. Joe is my cousin. I should be—'

'Hey, fiery one.' Her mother caught her hand. 'I think you should go. That's why I want you in bed *now*. Because you'll be getting up so early tomorrow. You've got a cousin and a friend to find.'

26

Packing up

'Do you think I should take these?' Joe dangled a pair of rabbit traps in front of Biddy's nose. She could see little bits of fur on the rusty teeth. 'Ugh! Take them away.' She was helping Joe pack his things. If they left soon, she figured, they could get to the beach before lunch and her parents would be there with the ute. She knew they would be.

Biddy stood back from Joe's campfire and looked at his possessions spread out on the grass. It wasn't much

to have collected in a lifetime. 'I reckon you should take all your stuff, as much as we can carry.'

'I don't know.' Joe screwed up his face. He looked across at the mountains. 'I wish you could have seen our valley.'

'Maybe I will. Maybe we'll go there one day and have a memorial service for your mum.'

'A what?'

'A memorial. A special ceremony to talk about her life, and put up a cross saying who she was and where she lived.'

'I don't think Joycie would like that.' Joe tossed the traps back into the hut.

Devil had been pacing up and down since dawn. 'He knows I'm going,' Joe told Biddy. 'He's that smart. He knows everything.' Suddenly the dingo looked to the end of the valley and whined. 'What is it, boy?' Devil bolted towards the bush and then doubled back. His eyes were boring into Joe, drinking him in. 'What's wrong, Devil?' Joe fondled his ears, trying to calm him. 'I've never seen him like this, Biddy.'

'I reckon my mum and dad are coming, and he can hear them.'

Joe hugged Devil tight. 'I think he's saying goodbye. He knows he's got to go.' Devil broke away from Joe's grip and raced across the valley. He stopped at the edge of the bush and looked back at them for a few seconds. Then he tilted his head slightly, just a dip really, as if he was signing off, and melted into the scrub. Joe's voice was like the wind in the grass: 'Bye, Devil,' he whispered.

Biddy didn't know what to say. Joe slumped on the log, staring into the coals of their breakfast fire. Her head was spinning with the stories Joe had told her last night, and she sat staring too. Her mind kept racing ahead, trying to imagine what it was going to be like for Joe. He'd live with Irene and her family—*he'd feel so crowded*—he'd have to go to school—*it would be so noisy*—he'd have to fit in with people—*he'd hate having to wait*. It went on and on. There were so many things he didn't know about.

Bella came and stood between the two of them, both staring, lost in their thoughts.

And that's what Irene saw when she stepped into the valley: her cousin and her friend, like bookends, with the white pony between them.

27

Joe's surprise

Biddy and Irene clattered down the steps of the school bus, their bags bumping behind them.

'Bye, giggle pots. See you tomorrow for the last day of school!' The bus driver swung the bus around and headed back to town.

The girls started down the gravel track that led towards Biddy's house, picking their way carefully so that their heels always landed on the biggest possible stones. They called this game 'High Heels', and they zig-zagged along putting on the voices posh ladies in high heels would use. 'I say, Irene,' said Biddy as they passed the dam, 'wouldn't you just love to catch some frogs?'

'Oh yes, Biddy, indeed I would ... Look! There's a huge one!' Irene immediately forgot her snobby voice. 'Quick, Bid! Give me your lunch box!'

She plunged down the bank, then scrambled back up,

legs dripping, and sat the lunch box in the middle of the track.

'What a beauty!' Biddy peered at the huge green bull-frog, sprinkled with spots of gold. Irene crouched beside her.

'Aren't his eyes beautiful? We better let him go . . . '

The blast of a car horn made the girls scream and leap off the track. Irene's dad was leaning out the window of his old truck, laughing.

'You two are hopeless, I could have run you over and you wouldn't have noticed. Chuck your bags on the back and you can squeeze in here with Joe.'

Biddy slid along the seat. 'How're you going, Joe? You and Mick look like twins now your hair's started to grow.'

Joe smiled but he didn't say anything. His arms were folded around his ribs as though he was cold, but his eyes were dancing. His smile grew wider.

'What have you been up to?' Biddy poked him. 'Look at him, Irene. And your dad. There's something they're not telling us.'

Irene caught her father's eye. 'Where have you been, Dad?'

'Well, you know my right-hand man here.' Joe snorted. 'Well, him and I have been giving your folks a hand with the hay, Biddy. As you know—'

'Dad,' growled Irene. 'Get to the point.'

'Well, stop interrupting. I broke the belt on the slasher, so Joe and I had to drive over to Henderson's workshop to pick up a new one.'

'Is that all?' asked Biddy. Mr Henderson was nice, and he did have a kelpie called Holly who could climb trees, but visiting there was no big deal. 'Come on, tell us what you've been doing.'

'All right,' said Mick, as the truck rolled to a stop beside the shed. 'Hop out and we'll tell you.'

Biddy pushed Irene out the door and waited for Joe. He wriggled his bum across the seat, then stepped down carefully from the truck.

'Why are you holding your arms like that?' asked Biddy.

Joe was grinning. It was as though he was so happy he couldn't speak.

Mick grabbed the girls' bags off the back of the truck. 'You know Holly?' he asked. 'Mr Henderson's bitch. And you know that dog of the Jacksons? The heeler?'

Joe stepped towards Biddy. 'Look.' He held open his shirt. She could see a fluffy bundle of brown and white nestled against his chest. 'I got a pup.' He showed Irene. 'I got a pup.'

Biddy was dying to cuddle the puppy, but it looked so comfortable that she put her arm around Joe instead.

'I'm going to call her Molly,' he said. 'Devil was my wild dog and she will be my home dog.'

Biddy gazed across the paddocks. Bella was lazing under the cypress tree, flicking flies with her tail. Across the bay the purple mountains of the headland faded into the sky.

'Do you want to hold her, Biddy?' Joe handed her the pup and his smile was as sunny as the day.

Acknowledgements

My thanks to the following people for their help with this
book: Billy Dwyer and Louey Fleming for the image on page i,
Mary Haginikitas, Matt Caldwell, Rosalind Price,
Sue Flockhart, and my family, especially my father,
Don, who told me these stories.

*Here is a picture of Taffy, with Alison's father
giving his children a double-double dink!*

A note from Alison Lester

I grew up at Foster in South Gippsland, Victoria. Our farm was like Biddy's farm. The big open paddocks ran down to Corner Inlet, and the mountains of Wilsons Promontory were beyond that. Our family farmed cattle, and in those days they bought 'store' (skinny) cattle from all over the country and fattened them. My dad and Uncle Jack also leased the southern end of the Prom and used it as a cattle run. They left the cattle there in the winter, to feed on the bush; then they were mustered and brought home to sell.

I can't remember learning to ride a horse. I think I always could. Mum used to pass me to Dad as he rode by the house, and he sat me on a cushion on the pommel. This was probably before I could walk. Once I was riding by myself, I fell off more times than I can remember. I got so good at falling off that I often landed on my feet. I always held onto the reins; it was a long walk home if the horse went without me. My brother and sisters and I rode together on the farm. We didn't put saddles on very often as it was too much trouble; usually we just sat on a chaff bag. Dad made us use saddles when we were doing stock work.

STOCK WORK

Stock work involved rounding up the cattle to drench them, checking the calving cows, checking the water, and getting cattle out to sell. Sometimes we drafted cattle in the paddock, separating the fat ones out for market. Then we took them up to the yards, where they'd be loaded onto trucks. That was the best fun, because we had to single out particular ones: 'Let the first one go, stop the next three, let that steer with the white patch go through . . .' You had to be on your toes. Dad took great pride in handling the cattle as calmly as possible, so that they wouldn't get stressed.

PONY CLUB

I went to pony club when I was eight. Once a month I used to trot twelve kilometres there, attend pony club, and trot home. I must have been tired on those Sunday nights. Every year I went to the Foster Show and would enter every event I could. The night before I'd lie awake and dream of all the blue ribbons, but I'd be lucky if I came home with a third prize for the School Pony competition.

When I was about twelve, Dad broke in a horse for me. His name was Blue, and when I took him to the Foster Show, he won the Champion Hack in the Shire of South Gippsland. I loved that champion ribbon.

MY HORSES

My very first horse was Inky. Santa bought her for me when I was about five. She was a sweet little old shaggy Shetland who was so quiet we used to dress her up in a cardigan and socks. My next horse was Tammy, a little grey pony. I fell off her lots of times—she was a pretty slippery customer—and she was lots of fun. Then Blue was my horse for a long time, until I was in my mid-twenties. My next horse was one I bought myself when I was teaching at Alexandra. He was an Arabian, called Ben Fox. The family next door was looking for someone to ride Ben. I loved him and they sold him to me when I moved away.

My horse now is called Woollyfoot, and he's a big Clydesdale Thoroughbred cross. Woollyfoot has been to pony club and one-day events with my children, and he has been to events and hunted with me, and also been on some big rides in the bush on the high plains.

MUSTERING

The first time I went mustering in the bush was with my friend Christa on the Dargo High Plains. We put out salt and called 'Saaaalt'—just as Biddy does in the story—because it's lacking in the cattle's diet and they see it as a treat. We rode right out into the bush to find any cattle that were feeding in little grassy valleys, then drove them back to the holding paddock. It took us a few days' ride to drive them all down the road to Christa's farm.

I've done a lot of bushwalking on the Prom and other places, and I've come across lovely little valleys that you can easily imagine living in. When writing about Joycie, I thought about what you couldn't do without when you are in the bush. You always make sure you've got matches and something to keep them dry and something to burn to start a fire with when riding in the bush. In the saddlebags we carry food, spare string, a snake-bite bandage and a pocket knife. And you have to dress so that you're safe from the weather. Lots of the country on the high plains looks the same, so unless you really know your way around, it would be easy to get lost. It's very spooky mustering when it's snowing or foggy.

WRITING THIS STORY

I loved writing this story as it was very easy to lose myself in Biddy's world. I could describe what that world looked and felt like because I knew it so well. I would just close my eyes and imagine riding down the beach or rubbing down a horse at the end of a long day.

Riding on the beach is a lovely feeling, and the story about the quicksand is true. Taffy did get bogged in quicksand and was left, then came home during the night. The sand on the beach can become unstable where there is water running underneath the surface, from a creek flowing under the sand.

My ideas for stories come from everywhere. I'm a magpie and collect little bits of information and store them in my head. If you love writing or drawing, consider making it your job. You just have to keep doing it, every day, and you'll get better and better.

Alison Lester

About the author

ALISON LESTER is the well-known creator of many popular and award-winning children's books, many of which reflect her own country childhood. *The Quicksand Pony* was shortlisted for the National Children's Award, Festival Awards for Literature in 1998, and in 1999 was the winner of the WA Young Readers Book Awards. *The Snow Pony* was shortlisted for both YABBA and KOALA awards, reflecting its popularity with young readers of horse stories. Her picture book *Are We There Yet?* was the 2005 winner of the Children's Book Council of Australia Book of the Year, Picture Book Award. *Running with the Horses* was shortlisted in the 2010 CBCA awards, and in 2011 *Noni the Pony* shortlisted in the CBCA awards and was the winner of the ABIA Book of the Year Award for Younger Children.

Alison visits schools in Australia and has been a writer in residence and guest speaker at international festivals. She is involved in many community art projects, and travelled to Antarctica to run the Kids Antarctic Art Project. Alison spends part of every year travelling to remote Indigenous communities, using her books to help children and adults write and draw about their own lives.